I0598889

THE ASSASSIN'S MARK

SARAH MÄKELÄ
TAVIN SØREN

KISSA PRESS LLC

THE ASSASSIN'S MARK

EDGE OF OBLIVION, BOOK ONE

*An assassin becomes a protector as he enters a magical world...
all for the woman of his dreams.*

Brigit Ó Ruaidh is the sole heir to the Kingdom of Freehaven. While journeying to visit a lord, she learns her
parents have been murdered...and she's next. With assassins
after her, she tries to prevent her kingdom from falling into
anarchy. But as she sets her eyes on the throne, her world
gets turned upside down when she's rescued by a dangerous
man.

Edward Emerson is an assassin. His job is to kill those who
bring death and suffering to his world. When he finds
himself in another world protecting a princess he's seen in
his dreams, he vows to move heaven and earth to keep her
safe. In return, he hopes to find his way back home.

Another claimant to the throne blocks their way, and he will
risk everything to make his mark on Freehaven and carve
out power of his own. If Brigit and Edward don't work

together, they won't live long enough to see her reclaim her destiny...or for their love to blossom.

Editor: Word Vagabond

Cover Artist: A.C. James

ISBN-10: 1942873840

ISBN-13: 978-1-942873-84-6

1

BRIGIT

A gentle fog rolled over the lands, making the glow of the afternoon sun slightly hazy. The light played off the towering mountains, their jagged white peaks dominating the truly majestic untamed woodlands. Despite the warmth radiating from my surroundings, I still found it difficult to relax. Something had been bothering me for the past few hours, even though my guards and my maid seemed at ease. If I said anything, they might report to my parents that I was trying to shirk my diplomatic duties again. I didn't want to disappoint them, so I kept my mouth shut.

The wind carried the unmistakable scent of the region's revitalized forests, but the fresh air did little to soothe my nerves. The small group of royal bodyguards mingled around me as we let the horses rest. They'd brought us far into the countryside, and I refused to make the precious animals suffer because some lord was impatiently waiting for his princess to arrive.

Lord Flemming was my cousin thrice removed. Father had convinced me to visit him since my cousin was the only noble with strong fortifications on this side of the Alean Swamp. The swamp had been a massive river once. Now it stood as a testament to the wrath and arrogance of past rulers before my ancestors claimed the land as their own.

History wasn't my best subject, but my mind kept returning to those dark ages. Tales of mad kings and queens who bathed in the blood of their servants had been a fascination of mine growing up. The Alean Swamp was the only thing that remained from those days. It was a natural habitat for many local species and protected by the king. Criminals and outcasts called it home, but not many lasted more than a few years in there.

My guards broke out into laughter, and I glanced in their direction, trying to catch what was so funny. Truthfully, I didn't care. I only wanted this trip to be over with so I could return to my parents and enjoy the time I had left with them. They were grooming me to find a husband of my own, but I wasn't ready for that next step in my life. They'd been patient, but I wanted a relationship like they had: something true and passionate. How could I find that in an arranged marriage?

My stomach clenched, and a wave of nausea sickened me. Could that be the true reason I was visiting my cousin? Had they decided who I would spend the rest of my life with? Would I be the last to know who they'd chosen?

Tabitha hurried to my side, always eager to help. "Are you okay, Your Highness?"

I nodded, placing my hands over my abdomen as the churning sensations continued. The last thing I wanted was to attract attention. "Please, you don't have to be that formal out here." Not that my request mattered. Tabitha always erred on the side of formality. "I'm fine."

She opened her mouth to say more, but I drew my eyebrows together and scowled at her.

"How much longer, Sir Alan?" I asked the stocky knight nearby. Sir Alan, my former teacher, had become my right-hand man during my journey across the Kingdom of Freehaven.

Normally, he donned heavy plate armor and wielded a mighty broadsword. However, this journey required lighter armaments, so he'd settled for chainmail and a short sword. He looked out of his element to me, but he projected a strength that would make any bandit think twice before attacking us. "The horses will be rested in half an hour, Your Highness." He bowed his head to me. "The soft land here isn't kind to them. We can't push nearly as hard as when we are on firm ground," he said, his baritone voice carrying easily in the fresh air.

"I understand. Thank you." I walked away from the group with my maid trailing after me. I disliked being looked after like some precious jewel. Back at the castle, I enjoyed my suite of rooms and spent much time reading and learning about my people. When the day finally came for me to take over, I wanted to be the leader this kingdom needed.

In the distance, the Alean Swamp stretched out before us. A heavy mist rose up from the swamp, continually blanketing the region in a dense, reddish fog creating an air of darkness and mystery. The commoners told of witches who had abandoned their white magick ways and preyed on villages bordering the swamp. Even my royal bodyguards seemed more on edge the closer we came to it and stayed near the horses whenever we took breaks. These were frequent as the landscape made this journey quite slow.

My advisors had recommended taking the popular

route across the mainland bridges, but that would have taken weeks. The constant buzz of mosquitoes was an annoyance, but it was better than dealing with the pomp and cheerful socializing I'd have to engage in on the normal road.

I'd insisted on the less-traveled shortcut, which would take a mere seven days. None of the group had been pleased with my decision. Sir Alan's face had gone bright red, and I'd thought he might pass out for a moment. He did his best to talk me out of my decision, but I remained steadfast. If I needed to visit my cousin, we would take as little time as possible doing it.

Still, I wasn't stupid. While the quiet route guaranteed anonymity, it brought its own share of danger. However, I wanted to be myself for a change, and not just Freehaven's princess. The outdoors gave me a glimpse of freedom and—like the fresh breeze—it was utterly welcome. I didn't even mind that I wore a heavy cloak to mask my identity and 'ensure my safety.' How crazy was that?

No one had threatened the nobility for decades. The general mood of the middle and lower classes was contentment. Outside of our realm, we had no political opponents that I was aware of. All of our neighbors had a long-lasting peace with us. The only thing this cloak protected me from was the barrage of insects. Not that I minded. I swatted one away as it buzzed near my face.

The distant sound of beating hoofs drew my attention toward the direction we'd come. Tabitha gingerly led me back to the bodyguards, who were staring at the newcomer just becoming visible over a low rise. The man and his horse both bore the royal colors. My knees shook, and I held on to Tabitha.

"Looks like a messenger from the royal court, Your Highness." Sir Alan's voice sounded grim even to my own ears. "Perhaps there's news from home."

I didn't trust myself to speak. I could only nod. The knot in my stomach balled up that much tighter, and I focused on breathing in the crisp, fresh air. My parents rarely sent word during my travels. The few times they had, there had been problems. If they were doing so now, it couldn't be good. Why had I let them talk me into traveling again?

"Don't look so concerned, princess. I'm sure all is well." Sir Alan strode away from the rest of us, toward the incoming horseman. Before he could make it far, the messenger wailed the news like a banshee, "They're dead. The king and queen are dead."

His words punched me in the gut, and my legs gave out. The ground hurtled toward me, but Tabitha's firm grip lessened its impact.

When my vision cleared, I blinked my eyes open to see Tabitha and Sir Alan hovering over me. "Wh-what happened? Why am I on the ground?"

Tears trailed down Tabitha's face, and I swore I saw moisture in Sir Alan's eyes. Dread washed over me. It was true then. I hadn't imagined the messenger's news. His voice still rang out in my ears, and I pushed into a sitting position to see him talking with the knights near the horses.

"Maybe you should rest for a moment, Your Highness." Tabitha exchanged a glance with Sir Alan, who was trying to keep me on the ground. "You just received terrible news. Your blessed parents..." Tabitha leaned her head forward and brushed the tears from her cheeks.

"What happened to them? Sir Alan? You have to tell me."

He frowned at me, keeping his gaze averted. "As Tabitha said, there's news of your parents. They..." He paused for a moment and let out a breath. "They've been murdered. Goddess rest their souls."

At his words, I ceased struggling to climb to my feet. It didn't feel worth it anymore. Nothing did. Numbness settled into my chest, and I turned my gaze skyward. How could the Goddess betray us like this? My parents were devout and loyal believers, always mindful to follow Her ways and provide a good example to the kingdom. If they had been murdered...what good was it to try to appease Her if bad things happened regardless of my parents' fair actions?

"Y-your Highness?" Tabitha placed a tentative hand on my arm and shook me a little as if I'd fallen asleep. No, I was very much aware of what had been said.

"Leave me for a moment." If I was going to deal with people, I needed to collect myself. If I'd learned anything, it was that I must always show strength as a leader. People looked for signs of weakness. "Once I'm ready, we will set off for my cousin's stronghold at once."

Tabitha opened her mouth as if to question my order, but she quickly stood and walked a few paces away.

Sir Alan, on the other hand, leveled a stare at me as he rose to his feet. "Stay strong, princess. Your kingdom relies on you now. We will find out who killed them, but you must remember that sometimes life takes us in unexpected directions." He shook his head. "Perhaps this is yours. It's up to you to decide what you to do with it."

I clenched my hands into fists at my sides beneath the heavy cloak. "Perhaps."

"I'll ready the horses then. We can't push them too harshly, but they'll have to bear it for now." He started to turn away, then glanced back at me. "You're already making wise decisions. It's better that we ride for your cousin rather than return home before we've assessed the situation. Your cousin has enough troops to protect you, and a sturdy castle."

"Let's not get ahead of ourselves. I don't plan on staying with Lord Flemming for long. I will return home to reap vengeance on those responsible for the deaths of Freehaven's king and queen." Since it didn't seem like I'd be getting the moment to myself, I pushed to my feet. He'd viewed my plans of seeing my cousin as more strategic than I had meant them. My desire had been for the comfort of court and the information found within. Regardless, we were sitting ducks here, ripe for killing. My knees still shook, but I pushed my shoulders back and lifted my chin, trying to think of how my mother would've acted in this situation.

Sir Alan merely bowed his head before turning away and returning to the group of knights and horses. The other guards were staring in my direction as they spoke in low voices. That made it all even worse. They were either trying to protect my feelings, or protect themselves from my anger. Regardless, I didn't care what they thought now.

I'd have enough of people talking about me in front of my face when I reached my cousin's. I faced away from the group, as if looking out over the majestic mountains, and merely focused on breathing until Sir Alan called out to the group about our imminent departure. The only thing I could do was carry on as my parents had taught me. They had ruled the land long before I was born. Thanks to their training, I knew what to do. Now I just needed to act.

2

EDWARD

The day had been relatively quiet until the phone started ringing. Life was calm and almost normal while I was between assignments. Not all covert agents lived the high life like James Bond. I sat on the couch in my London flat and kicked my feet up on the matching beige ottoman. The annoying call interrupted the Manchester United game I'd recorded, one of the few things I enjoyed outside of work.

I answered the phone with a crisp, "Yes?"

"Edward, I sincerely apologize for interrupting, but something has come up," Croft said cautiously from the other end of the line. This didn't bode well. Croft handled my assignments, and he rarely ever rang me. Most of our encrypted communication was through e-mail or text messaging. He never saw the urgency to do more than that, unless things weren't going well. His wary tone also threw me off. Our team rarely showed that kind of vulnerability to one another. We were trained to be strong and fearless.

"What's the latest, Croft?" The nagging feeling in the pit of my stomach grew in size. "Is everyone at the office safe?" I lowered my voice a little and turned up the television in case anyone was listening in. All interest I'd had in the game was gone now as I waited for Croft to gather his notes and give me a brief rundown on whatever was happening.

"They're fine. However, a target of yours has surfaced again. We have footage of the man behind the bombings in Berlin last month. He's presently in London. I know you're off-duty, but I have a bad feeling about his presence here. You're needed out there, mate."

I clenched my hand into a fist. The man behind those bombings was mine to catch. He'd eluded me, something a rare few had done. "I'll look into it. Send me the details."

The clacking of his keyboard preceded a chime on my phone. "Done."

"Keep me updated if anything changes." I hung up the phone, then changed clothes. Within ten minutes, I was headed out the door and on my way to the terrorist's last known location.

The smell of gasoline and the unwashed bodies of a few homeless people to my left rankled my nose as I strode through the seething underbelly of London. I'd been given a clue as to what my target was up to—not much of one, but enough to act upon. He was last seen at a local market buying some ingredients for what seemed to be an explosive device. Aerosol containers of hair spray, a box of nails, a couple of digital timers, cleaning chemicals, and a few pots and pans had been enough to cause the store clerk to ring up the hotline with a tip. Security footage outside of the shop had confirmed the target's identity.

My suit was perfectly tailored to conceal my Sig P938 and a tactical knife. With a quick mental check on the surrounding streets, I slowed my pace.

I approached the tenement building from the west for a

better look. The terrorist didn't work alone, so I knew to anticipate lookouts and other flunkies. A man leaned against a wall opposite from the building. He wasn't doing a good job of masking his presence. He kept scanning the alleys leading toward one particular staircase. The man's general demeanor gave him away as he failed to act natural. His jumpy reactions and shaky frame told me he was using chemical assistance to remain alert.

My time was limited. I had little choice but to take him out. The alleyway was well-hidden and quiet with the occasional sound of laughter from the nearby school barely reaching it. Not wanting to draw much attention, I pulled my knife and held it against my side as I walked toward the man. I held my cell phone to my ear, taking advantage of the fact that people rarely paid attention to a person on the phone. The man was too agitated to notice me. He kept his gaze on the alley as if his life depended on it, which allowed me to get close.

With a swift elbow to the face, I sent the man flailing into the alley beside us. He fell against the wall, and I slashed my blade across his throat, careful not to get sprayed by his blood. Messy but silent. That summed up my job, really. We were trained for these situations, taught things like how to angle a knife when slicing someone's throat and how to pull it away to avoid ruining your clothes and drawing attention to yourself. All manner of oddly useful information.

The man struggled for a few moments, but as the light faded from his eyes, he slumped over.

I wiped the blade clean on the hem of his shirt, then rummaged through his pockets to find a key with a number tag on it. *Gotcha!* This was working out nicely. I rearranged the trash bags to conceal his body. He wouldn't be found for hours.

After taking a few moments to be sure there were no other guards around, I finally began my approach. The numbers on the key guided me toward the correct flat. A couple of stairs later, I stood beside a heavy metal door, in a hallway with no windows and a narrow walkway. The out-of-service lift was stuck, its doors repeatedly trying to open and close behind me. I stayed quiet, doing my best to listen to my surroundings and piece together what was taking place. Everyday sounds of talking or television came from several of the flats. Something felt off about all of this.

Shite.

I headed down to the second floor and called Croft to inform him of the situation. This was exactly like what had happened in Berlin. The terrorist had tried to kill as many people as he could with his bombs placed at a crowded kinder-garten. There were several tenement buildings here with a school nearby. A serious amount of explosives could be in the lift between floors where the terrorists could freely access it in middle of the night. Croft told me that there were at least five people in the flat where my target was. Any one of them could have the trigger, and the lift itself could be trapped.

"Of course. On a bloody Monday," I grumbled under my breath after hanging up.

The process was clear: evacuate the building, disarm the explosive, and get rid of the threat. The last two sometimes took care of themselves, but more often than not, it was better to deal with the explosive before taking out hostiles.

The threat's close proximity to the school made my skin crawl. To hell with the procedure. If they caught wind that something was wrong, who knew what they'd do. Locating a maintenance door to the lift shaft took only a few moments. At least the maintenance man had left a spare hoist way key nearby, which I put into my pocket.

The lift itself rested on the cables several feet down from where I was. The ladder would give me access to the elevator, but I didn't trust it. What if it was booby-trapped? I grabbed the cables and slowly slid down to the lift's roof.

With sore hands, I opened the hatch on top and took a cursory glance inside. Through the darkness, I could faintly make out the shape of pressure containers, gas bottles resting against tins, and closed containers littering the floor. A few red lights here and there showed that some of the makeshift bombs were powered, making them dangerous to disarm. I wasn't exactly a trained bomb tech, but I knew enough. Using my flashlight to scan the packages, I couldn't discern any pattern, organization, or other reason for the materials to be spread around inside the lift as they were. Extensive sets of wires ran to and from a small box beneath what seemed to be an acetylene gas container.

I tucked my feet beneath the support bar holding the cables and lowered my head and torso inside the lift, being careful not to touch anything. With the flashlight in my mouth, I did my best not to grimace as I hunted for the section of explosive that mattered the most: the remote detonator. With the reinforced metal of the lift acting like a Faraday cage, it wasn't hard to find. Thick wires were running out of the lift's main body and outside of it. The detonator had even been wired to some of the control panels inside the main cage to ensure the device's batteries were fully charged.

All in a day's work.

I reached for a smaller utility knife on my belt, all of my movements slow and careful. I peeled off the protective layer on the antenna cable, making sure not to touch the conductive wiring inside. First, I'd have to check if this thing was protected by an active signal. With no voltmeter, I touched the wire to the tip of my tongue and waited. Nothing happened. No jolts of any kind. Satisfied, I followed the wire around the lift's walls with a flashlight. A small copper wire betrayed the locations where the cable was taped to the roof nearby, easy enough to access. With remote detonation disabled, I took my time and snipped the cable, while focusing my eyes on the red LED lights that glowed around me.

To my immediate relief, none of them flashed as I cut the wire. That was one less thing to worry about. As I returned for my target, I spotted a man outside of the suspected terrorists' door with a bag of groceries in his arms. He wasn't my primary target, but when I spotted the keys in his hand, I realized he'd still be helpful. He barely registered my presence as he balanced the heavy bag with one arm while trying to get the key into the lock.

With my tactical knife in hand and a clear path to my objective, I let my instincts take over. I used one arm to support his weight as I stabbed him in the neck, pointing the blade upward into his skull. The poor bastard only managed a soft whimper before he dropped dead against me. Dragging him and the bag of groceries away without a sound took some effort, but in the end, I would be able to complete my mission with one less person in the way. I hid his body hastily and leveraged the grocery bag for visual cover as I opened the door.

"Amir, you are late. Did you get everything?" A male voice came from an adjoining room as soon as I stepped inside the flat. The low voice carried a Turkish accent, which matched my target's nationality.

The hallway's shaggy carpet was full of stains, and the rest of the entry wasn't in much better shape. I saw two large roaches scurrying along the walls, as if looking for a place to hide. The chances of them using this as an ongoing hideout were slim. Plain walls and empty built-in bookshelves reinforced the fact these men were here to cause terror, soon, and then move on.

I dodged into the kitchen to avoid being seen. The bag might work for a moment, but it wouldn't be useful for long. I left the groceries on the counter and turned in time to see a man walk into the room. Thinking on my feet, I threw my knife, catching him in the throat. I glanced into the hallway to see a man's shadow ducking out of the view.

There goes the element of surprise.

I rolled to the small bedroom on the other side of the hall, wiping the blade on the dirty carpet before putting it away. The knife wouldn't help me now. I drew my gun from its shoulder holster. From the end of the hallway where I'd seen the shadow, I heard hushed whispers, just before gunfire opened up on the kitchen's wall. Bullets pierced the wall in short, controlled bursts, in search of their target.

I glanced into the hall and squeezed off two shots into the shooter's chest. It might not kill him, but I hoped it would be enough to keep him out of my way. If Croft's intel was right, with two targets down, three were still in the flat.

The bedroom had a door within it that presumably led to a bathroom. I'd seen this type of floor plan before, and if I was right, the bathroom would connect to the second bedroom. The soft creak of the hinges on the bathroom's door put me on edge. As I'd hoped, a second door stood before me, and I crept closer to the other bedroom. Whispers came from the other side, but this time I could listen in better. There were at least three targets. None of them spoke English.

I turned the handle ever so slightly to gauge its stiffness, then sprang into action. A quick twist of the knob and four steps took me into the thick of things. By then, I had my gun aimed.

I shot the man closest to me as he began to aim at my chest, then threw my knife into the farthest guy's chest. The last man standing, my main target, moved to the left to swing his rifle around. His finger was locked around the trigger. *Rookie mistake.* With his stiff tracking stance, he lacked mobility. I slid toward him on the laminate floor, letting my momentum carry me closer. He tried to keep me in his sights, but the rifle's size was too much for such close quarters. There was no way he'd be able to reliably hit me, and once he took a shot, he'd have to manually reload the gun before being able to try again. That made him hesitate.

I fired into his right knee, sending his shot wide. Another bullet ripped into his left arm and made him drop his rifle. My weapon remained trained on him as I rose to my feet. "We've finally caught you, you bloody bastard," I said aloud, scanning the room to make sure no one else was hostile.

The one I'd shot twice in the chest stared up at the ceiling with wide, unblinking eyes. The rest of them moaned in pain, but they didn't move around much. For a brief moment, I let my guard down. The tables in the room held various pots and pans, two scales, and a few boxes of nails beside empty cylinders that betrayed their intent well enough. Among the items were zip ties. *Useful.* I used them to tie the arms and legs of my target and his friends. It might take time for support to arrive, but this way they wouldn't get themselves into much trouble while we waited. I still needed to secure the building and get any civilians out of there.

Satisfied the situation was under control, I walked into the hall and pulled the fire alarm. Anyone here would get the hint to leave the building until help came.

I pulled my phone out to ring Croft as I walked back inside the terrorists' flat. The alarm blared, and nervous residents filed out of their flats in a hurry. "Job's done. The residents are fleeing the building now. Send some support to get these guys into custody."

"Good work. Police will be there shortly since someone called them about the fire alarm. Stand by." Croft sounded quite pleased, and all was right with the world again. Maybe I could finish watching the football match soon. I already knew who won, but that didn't matter.

A polite knock from the flat's front door made me turn around cautiously, tucking my phone away. The brief outline of my attacker came into view just before a fire extinguisher struck me. My body felt weightless as I collapsed to the ground. Our intel had been wrong. Another bomber lived here too.

"Fucking MI6," I heard as I blacked out.

3

BRIGIT

As we arrived at Lord Flemming's stronghold, I remained quiet, paying little attention to the usual pomp and circumstance of court. It was hard enough dealing with the aching loss in my chest and the knowledge that my beloved parents were dead.

My gaze rose to see my cousin standing in the courtyard, apparently waiting for me. His eyes were slightly puffy and bloodshot. Apparently, the news had been hard on him, too. If it weren't for my parents, Lord Flemming wouldn't be where he was today. They'd treated him almost like a son when his own parents abandoned and betrayed him.

Sir Alan and Tabitha supported me with their presence through the usual court ceremony I was expected to participate in. I held back my tears as best I could. Royalty had no public outlet for these kinds of emotions. Outrage, fury, and hatred were all seen in the royal court at times, but sorrow and loss were private affairs. In its own way, the frivolous façade forced me to focus my mind on the here and now, not on what just happened. My plate would be overflowing with tasks to handle over the next few days. The list of requirements for the Kingdom of Freehaven to remain stable was long.

I needed to make speeches and attend ceremonies...and go through the coronation to be crowned the new queen. The normal expectations for an heir to gain the throne were magnified, especially now that my family's direct lineage dangled by my life's thread. Soon I'd need to marry and provide the kingdom with an heir.

Nausea roiled my stomach, and I pushed those thoughts aside. The princess's headdress was heavy enough. Was I actually ready to become my kingdom's monarch?

Eventually the greetings and exchange of pleasantries ended, and my cousin and I were able to escape to a private meeting chamber with a selection of other nobles from the area. As we departed the opulent great hall, I felt like I could take a deep breath for the first time since I'd arrived.

The heavy oak doors closed behind me, separating us from the rest of the court. Without all the pageantry, my thoughts strayed back toward my parents. The sting of tears burned my eyes, but I held them back. Now wasn't the time to cry. I'd do that later, when I reached my suite of rooms.

Sir Alan nodded toward the end of the long table. He hadn't left my side since we'd learned of the news. That was partly due to the threat to the kingdom's stability if I died too, but he'd also been my teacher as a child, and a friend to my parents. His warm presence made me feel like I wasn't alone.

My cousin sat at the opposite end of the table from me, and I looked at the solemn men gathered in the room. They were locked in debate over military strategy to secure me my throne.

Sir Alan had sent for bread and wine, since we hadn't eaten for several hours. The journey here had taken precedence, and it would be awkward if my stomach began growling now.

The noblemen argued over the most minute details, everything from how strong the force should be to who we could really trust and when we would leave.

I spoke up where I could, but the majority of their bickering went right over my head. My father had taken me to similar discussions before, but they'd never interested me. There was never a reason to pay attention, because I knew he would take care of the kingdom and lead us to victory.

The nobles kept rehashing the same strategies and details over and over without coming to an agreement. When they talked about the latrine details for the third time, I'd finally had enough. There was more to moving an army than I'd realized. However, if we stood any chance of making this work, we should be unifying and coming together, not fighting amongst ourselves like this.

"I think a smaller force might be optimal. It would avoid unwanted attention and allow us to scout out the capital. Perhaps then we wouldn't need to mobilize our armies," I said. No one appeared to pay me any attention. They kept shouting each other down. Sir Alan slammed his fist on the heavy oak table to my right, nearly making me jump out of my skin, but it drew everyone's attention. The noblemen all quieted down and stared at him with widened eyes. The moment passed by too quickly, and then all of the men started up again, with vigor.

Objections and outrage rained down from all sides of the room at once. Several of the nobles were adamant about having their colors flown, to show those in the kingdom that they supported the crown. Others agreed that secrecy and stealth were paramount.

My head began to ache from all the arguing around me.

The only two people in the room whose opinions mattered to me were Sir Alan's and my cousin's, both of whom now knew how I felt about the matter.

"Silence, you fools! My cousin is the princess of Freehaven, and soon she'll be your queen! I demand you show her some respect." Lord Flemming never was one to mince his words.

I gave him a soft smile. I'd been wrong to not want to visit him. At least I was here now.

"There are advantages to her idea that you lot seem to be missing," an elder voice said from the far corner of the table. The older man wore the sigil of the tutors who advised the royalty in all manners of old knowledge, warfare, and politics. "We received news that her parents didn't just die. They were assassinated. They were known by all to have bodyguards wherever they went." He rose to his feet from where he'd been seated and scratched his chin. "It'd be logical to assume that whoever killed them would not hesitate to go after our lovely princess under similar circumstances. She is wise to want to move around quietly. The people of Freehaven will take the news of their king and queen's murder harshly as we've already seen at this stronghold. The last thing they need is the death of their princess. I'd be inclined to agree with Her Highness. A small company of knights and a few servants will do better than raising all of our banners and making a long march to the capital."

The elder spoke in an even tone, as if he knew his opinion mattered to the men in the room. He exchanged a look with my cousin, and it was evident his loyalty was more to Lord Flemming than me. That mattered little right now. Let them play politics amongst themselves. I just wanted this over and done with so I could return home, where I was needed most.

Sir Alan leaned in close to whisper into my ear. "You need to declare your will. The stronger you make yourself look now, the more the men around this table will respect you. The army's details can be discussed in private, since I'm sure you're overwhelmed, but you need to take the reins on this discussion before it gets more out of control." His patient voice reminded me of times past when he'd taught me how to wield a sword.

He was right. I needed to step up. I couldn't let this group of men rule me. This was my destiny and my birthright. I rose to my feet, and the room quieted again.

"I appreciate your guidance through this tough time. Each of you may know what you think is best. However, I believe in my heart that a smaller group will travel more quickly and draw less attention from possible assassins. We cannot afford to show fear to whomever has committed the horrible act that ended my parents' lives. We are not scared, nor are we vulnerable. The best use of our soldiers will be using our armies to wipe out the forces of the person who orchestrated their deaths. Sir Alan will discuss the specifics with you and make arrangements for my departure home. The throne needs to be secured." My knees trembled a little as all of their eyes fixed on me, but I held my chin up and tried to portray a strength I didn't feel right then and there. My gaze remained on my cousin, who gave me the barest hint of a smile to encourage me. "Thank you for your cooperation and assistance, my lords."

I expected the noblemen around the table to begin arguing again immediately. Instead, they bowed their heads to me and murmured their approval to one another.

My heart pounded in my chest as I walked out of the private meeting chamber. Perhaps I could find something else to eat before I retired for the evening. Sir Alan would likely want us to depart at first light. I glanced back into the room and caught my cousin's eye. I still hoped to speak with him alone before I left.

I wasn't sure when we'd be able to see each other again. Traveling wouldn't be safe until we caught whomever had killed my parents. Lord Flemming might very well have a target on his back, too. He was in the line of succession, after all. Granted, not close enough to where I was immediately fearful of his life. We had other family floating about that neither of us really talked with.

The servants in my cousin's stronghold were friendly and smiled at me, although I could see the sadness in their eyes. Tabitha, my maidservant, found someone from the kitchen to fix me supper. Bread and wine were great, but I needed more than that.

"Would you like the food brought to your suite room or to the dining hall, Your Highness?" a maid said as she curtsied.

I opened my mouth to reply, but a masculine voice spoke up behind me. "The dining hall would suit us."

"My Lord." The maid looked between me and Lord Flemming, as if unsure what to do.

"Yes, the dining hall please."

She curtsied again before leaving.

"I'm glad you're well. That was one of the hardest meetings I've seen. I apologize for the nobles. They aren't used to this type of stress. It's a lot to plan for with very little warning." He brushed a strand of hair from my face. "I only wish you could stay longer. I know the importance of you returning home, but I feel uneasy knowing you'll be in danger. Please have word sent back when you arrive. I would like to witness your crowning."

"Yes, I'll be sure to do that." I glanced around the hallway, but the crowd had dispersed as the evening stretched on. Many were likely still gathered in the grand hall or had retired to their rooms. "Be careful. You're my family. No one is sure yet what the assassin hopes to achieve. I'd be devastated to lose you too."

Lord Flemming wrapped his arm around my shoulder and led me toward the dining hall. "I'll be sure to keep that in mind." He smiled at me. "It's nice to know you care."

I playfully pushed at his arm. "You should know I do."

"Why is it I've heard that my sweet cousin wasn't terribly excited to come visit then?" He grinned, and the smile shone through his eyes. I couldn't help but fall into his piercing green gaze.

"Well, it's a long journey. Your stronghold isn't conveniently located in respect to our kingdom's capital." I leaned into his arm as we walked down the hallway together, feeling the strong warmth of his presence. For the first time today, I was truly able to relax.

"I'll have to keep that in mind, Your Highness," he said, laughter in his voice. "Perhaps I'll visit you in Darkview when things settle down, instead of holding out hope of seeing you back here."

"I'll be queen. Of course you should!" We laughed together and continued talking for a few hours. I'd be exhausted in the morning, but that didn't seem to matter much now.

4

EDWARD

I blinked my eyes open on an unexpected landscape. The gentle, rolling hills reminded me of Ireland. Lush deep green grass blanketed the ground as the vibrant hues of the forest beyond stirred my interest. Clean air filled my lungs, and I pushed into a sitting position. None of my travels had prepared me for *her*.

A lovely young woman in a thin shift stood in the midst of a nearby field. Her delicate form took my breath away, and her saddened expression made my heart ache. Everything within me wanted to go to her, protect her. Thunder rumbled in the distance, bringing with it an edge of danger, but the only thing I could focus on was her solemn beauty.

Part of me knew this was just a dream, but I didn't want to turn away from her and wake up. Rain clouds darkened the sky above us. The field lit up as flashes of lightning struck the ground near her.

I held up a hand to shield my eyes and stumbled to my feet. If she didn't get out of there, she'd die.

The young woman lifted her face to the sky, tears streaking her cheeks.

She needs you. A middle-aged woman's voice fluttered through my head, urging me toward the younger lady. *Her time has come. He'll kill her if you don't act.*

I turned in a full circle, but I was alone now, with storm clouds overhead. This couldn't be happening to me. This was beyond surreal. It had happened before, but this was nothing like that experience. The sense of urgency I felt drove me to act. What was going on?

As soon as I began questioning the scene around me, a sharp pain jolted me back to the present. I touched the back of my head, and blood dampened my fingers. The fire extinguisher flashed back to my mind. I'd been hit. Still, that didn't exactly explain the odd vision.

One moment I was in a wonderful, green paradise with a nearly naked, young woman, and the next I was in what was presumably someone's basement, my face pressed against dirty concrete and a foot jammed into my lower back. *Fucking shite.* At least he didn't think to bind my arms. I had something going for me.

The foot didn't budge, and the man it belonged rattled off something in Turkish into a cell phone. Maybe he hadn't felt me stir beneath him, or maybe he simply didn't care. I moved my left hand to my pocket for the blade I'd shoved there after the fight earlier, more than a little surprised he hadn't taken it. I jabbed the knife into my assailant's kneecap.

He yelled in surprise and pain as he stumbled away from me, releasing the pressure on my back.

I scrambled to my feet and caught sight of the terrorist. He had a scruffy beard, angry black eyes, and flared nostrils. He didn't have the presence of a leader. He was a grunt, probably waiting on someone to tell him when to proceed. I threw a few mock punches to get his guard up and backed him into a corner where I kicked him in his already wounded knee.

An audible snap reverberated through the room as the tendons gave way. I barely paid attention to his snarl or the pained expression on his face. Instead, I threw all my might into a solid punch to his jaw. Sloppy, but it did the trick. His head bounced against the wall behind him, and he dropped to the floor.

I darted to the nearby door and turned the knob. The moment the doorknob twisted, I knew something was wrong. Electricity bit my fingers and gave off a sharp, snapping sound. Horror washed over me as I realized what he'd done. He'd booby-trapped our only escape. Time would tell how long I had until my demise.

I snatched my possessions from the floor, preparing for what was to come, but no footsteps rang out nearby, and no one barged into the basement.

Unfazed, I glanced around at the grey concrete and spotted a place where builders had done recent repairs. With a few tentative knocks, I found an empty cavity. They'd been building several bombs in the flat I'd raided. Of course, they'd have multiple targets here in London. Damn it. Taking inventory of the room, I noticed a set of heavy-duty tools and felt a pang of relief. Hammer, just what I needed. I grabbed it and smashed the wall.

As I broke through the hastily patched construction, I saw the outline of a large metal door. A sharp glint in the thick dust caught my eye, and I reached for it without thinking. The large skeleton key seemed out of place in this day and age. It had a somewhat Gothic look, with a stylized skull-and-crossbones decoration. How long had this been down here? Judging from the thickness of the dust, it could have been decades, if not centuries.

I shoved the key into my pocket and turned to leave, but a muffled explosion from another side of the basement kicked my instincts into high gear. I darted to the heavy door and pulled, but it was locked. For a few moments, the animalistic part of my brain jerked on the handle in desperation, hoping it was simply stuck, then rational thinking came to the rescue.

I pulled the key from my pocket and shoved it into the lock. Blood trickled from my hand where the key's decoration cut into my skin, but I hardly noticed. The click from the lock rang true. My heart leapt, and I yanked the door open.

The doorway didn't reveal what I'd expected, which was a staircase up toward the street. I was confused, but only for a moment. Then the world slowed as a blast of hot air from the explosion threw me forward into the green fields beyond the door, and everything went black.

Time passed in the darkness of my head. Fleeting scenes from my previous dream rolled through my mind—the alluring, young woman's shape as she waited in the green fields for the storm, the constant rumbling of thunder in the background. The driving need to keep her safe plagued my uneasy mind. Like a fever dream, the scenes played repeatedly, relentlessly, until the darkness returned.

Dripping rain splashed against my cheek and finally drew me back to my senses. Every muscle in my body ached, and every time I moved, I had to focus on not passing out. *Simple goals.*

My first priorities were shelter and warmth. The blast had slightly singed my hair and my skin, but it seemed I'd escaped the worst of it. I rolled over onto my back, instantly regretting the decision as pain radiated up my spine. Any idea on how to return home was beyond me at the moment.

I was in a field surrounded by rolling hills and forests. In the distance was a majestic mountain range. Not exactly something one would expect to see in the United Kingdom, but I wasn't intimately familiar with the countryside. How did I get here? I'd come through a door, but there were no buildings around. I pushed to my feet and started to gather small twigs and patches of grass as I scanned my surroundings.

I doubted that wherever I was I'd have any cell signal, but I checked anyway. Nothing. It seemed I'd have to press on in hopes of finding that door. Surely I'd find someone who knew where it was. Maybe I simply sleepwalked away from it after the explosion, though that seemed unlikely since walking was such a chore right now. Letting out a sigh, I returned to my goals. Shelter and warmth. I could figure out what was happening later.

It took about an hour for me to build passable shelter and to start a fire. The tactical knife was an immense help in both tasks. Thanks to the steadily falling rain, I wouldn't be running out of fluids for the moment, either. My injuries were mostly minor burns and scratches, but a few bruises on my left arm were large and extremely painful. They'd make life less than happy for the next few days. I doubted I'd find any creams to soothe my muscles out here.

The longer I stared at the scenery, the more familiar it appeared to be. It shared similar characteristics to Ireland or Scotland, but the woods and the plants were different. The air was warmer as well. It did little to lift my spirits, but at least I didn't have to worry about finding thicker clothing anytime soon. Winter was likely some time off, and with any luck, I'd be able to return home before then.

My shelter was at the base of a sturdy tree, but I perched on a branch high above the ground, protected from most predators. I remained close to the edge of the forest. The view across the clearing was incredible, and I thought I could see some kind of path or road in the distance. A few bugs buzzed through the air, but I didn't pay any attention to them. I leaned back against the solid trunk of the tree, grimacing a little before I settled in and closed my eyes.

Judging by the angle of the sun, early morning had turned to late afternoon by the time I finally woke. The branches beneath me stirred, as if something was foraging near the roots. I could see the broad outline of a bear sniffing my shelter. Climbing the tree had been a wise decision after all. Perhaps if I remained still, it wouldn't notice me. I turned my attention back to the road, where I spotted people traveling on horseback. Odd, but maybe not uncommon for somewhere out in the country. Part of me wanted to call out to them, but I couldn't do that. *Observe and act, never react.* My mentor's old saying usually proved invaluable. Not only did I have no clue where I was or if I could communicate with these people, but if I drew their attention, I might draw the bear's as well.

On the other hand, they might have food with them, and food was something I hadn't procured yet. Getting closer to the traveling group might take time, but time was something I had plenty of...I hoped. Fighting off pangs of hunger, I kept my gaze on the travelers, my ears focused on the grunting bear as it ate something in the bushes nearby. Surely he'd move on soon enough.

I waited for a good ten minutes after the bear left before climbing down the tree. I didn't want to waste precious ammo on a bear, and the knife would require getting far too close to it. Instead of running toward the road, I walked quietly, taking cover behind the shrubbery until I reached a small hill nearby. Dragging myself along on my stomach, I took my time in the high grass, making sure I wouldn't draw too much attention.

At the top of the hill, I stole a glance around the expanse of hills, which seemed to go on for miles. On one side was a darker, wetter forest that continued farther than I could see. A rolling fog rose from the trees. On the other side of the clearing were steep mountains with jagged cliffs. The road cut straight through the swamplands to the closest hillside before taking a sloped descent into grasslands.

Not far from me, the group of travelers I'd spotted before were riding along on their way. I followed them from a distance, but the more I really looked at them, the stranger all of this became.

The group looked like a troupe from a medieval faire. But unlike any faire I'd seen, these people appeared totally devoted to authenticity. Wherever I'd ended up didn't appear to be anywhere I was familiar with. People in the modern world didn't dress in medieval costume and tended to travel in cars. Where in the bloody hell was I? Or rather, *when* was I?

A small part of me toyed with the idea of dropping onto my back in the grass and giving up, but I wouldn't let self-pity take root inside me. I might miss the modern commodities I'd grown used to, but this group likely had food and a change of clothes I could 'borrow' to better blend in with this new area. Besides, someone might know where the damn door was to return home.

I released a soft sigh and kept pace with the group. Most of the men in chainmail appeared to be surrounding a rider who was completely engulfed in a large cloak that concealed their face. Whoever they were guarding seemed to be important enough to warrant a lot of muscle.

While I still had my firearm, it'd do little for me in the

long run. None of the guards appeared to have guns, so I doubted there would be gunsmiths in this area. That meant there might not be any molds to make bullet casings for additional bullets. There might be a chance for black powder, but it'd likely be unreliable compared to modern-day gunpowder. The last thing I wanted was to lose a few fingers. That meant I'd have to resort to melee fighting. Maybe the fencing lessons I'd taken as a lad would come in handy.

However, a modern-day fighter with a tactical knife confronting medieval swordsmen with longswords? I really didn't like my odds there.

5

BRIGIT

The trek back home seemed to be going slower than I'd hoped. My guards didn't want to rush our trip, favoring vigilance over speed. While I appreciated their concern, I had pressing matters back home. Besides, I didn't like crawling along at a snail's pace. I didn't have the military background they did, but in my opinion, we were painting more of a target on our—*my*—back by taking our time.

Still, I was exhausted from staying up so late with my cousin last night. I'd barely managed an hour of sleep, but it was nice catching up with him. I couldn't stop kicking myself that I'd been so reluctant to visit in the first place. However, a dark thought lingered at the back of my mind that maybe if I'd stayed home my parents would still be alive. I couldn't dwell on it. Those ideas would just drive me closer to insanity.

Sir Alan remained quieter than he'd been on our trip to see Lord Flemming. He kept looking over his shoulder, on our left, as if someone was out there. "Your Highness, I have a feeling that we're being followed. Perhaps we should set up camp soon. That way I can chase off whoever is disturbing us, and you may get some rest." He scowled at me. "You shouldn't have remained awake until the wee hours of the morning. It wasn't responsible."

"That was my decision to make. While it might not please you, I'm an adult capable of thinking for myself. I needed that time—"

"That may be the case, princess, but you're tired. When you're tired, you are weak." Sir Alan's frown deepened. "You've been stifling yawns all day, and a few times I've seen you nearly fall asleep atop your horse. Your safety is my concern and my priority. If nothing else, do me a favor and get plenty of rest while we're camped. You need to be alert and able to defend yourself against any threat we might face, just as I trained you. You may not always have guards around to look after you. If it comes to that, you need to survive for your kingdom." He bowed his head to me. "You may not like my words, but I need you to respect them. It may be our only hope." With that, he spurred his horse on to speak with the knights currently leading the group.

I gritted my teeth and did my best not to ball my hands into tight fists on the reigns. My horse usually sensed my moods, and it was all I could do to keep my nerves calm enough after the news of my parents dying. The mare didn't need any more distractions from me. What bothered me most about Sir Alan's comments was that I knew in his way he was right. I'd acted selfishly when I really needed to be thinking of the kingdom and staying safe. If an assassin did jump out at us right now, I'd probably be too tired to do much. I relied so much on the fact I had guards that I barely had a plan if they were to be killed. If I were left without protection, what would I do?

"He's right, you know, Your Highness. However, you

shouldn't torture yourself." Tabitha had remained a constant at my side during this whole trip. Whenever I needed anything, she was there to provide it. "You needed to see your cousin. It's only natural that you wished to spend time with your family member." She offered me a gentle smile. "Don't take Sir Alan's words too harshly. He said them because he cares about you and the kingdom."

"I know. I need to make better decisions, to be the kind of ruler my parents were. It's just still hard to comprehend without being there. Truth be told, I'm not happy I had to visit my cousin in the first place, but I enjoyed talking with him. It made me feel like I wasn't all alone in the world." I shrugged a shoulder. "I know that might sound a little strange, but I'm not close to my other family. I barely know them, because of that silly falling out my mother had with one of my uncles. It strained things, but you learn that there are more important things in life than worrying about what others think. The ones who matter most are the ones you pay attention to."

"Wise advice, Your Highness."

After a few moments, we fell into a companionable silence. We'd passed through Skyhaven at the midpoint of our journey to my cousin's stronghold, so it was disappointing that we were still so far away. My nerves were wound tight in my hurry to return to my family's castle.

Everyone dismounted from their horses in the wide field, and a few of the servants started constructing the camp. The guards gathered together with Sir Alan in the middle of them for a brief meeting, after which some of them would help complete the camp's construction. Sir Alan glanced my way a few times, as if making sure I wasn't getting into trouble. It unnerved me a little, making me feel like a child who needed to be kept in line by a parent. I'd never really felt that way around him before, but this wasn't a typical time in my people's history. If we were going to make it through, I had to keep my chin up and be the person my parents had expected me to be.

I turned my back on him. I had more pressing matters right now. Beside me, Tabitha helped one of the servants set up my tent. I wished we were at Skyhaven so I could stay in one of the inns instead. It'd likely be safer for me there. The guards took turns watching over my tent and checking on my safety. Sir Alan also seemed to have organized a patrol routine to ensure the camp would remain secure during the evening. But who in their right mind would attack a camp full of knights? That was beyond me. I just didn't see the point.

Despite the alternative routes we'd taken and our quest to remain undetected, it seemed bad news always had a way to find us. The occasional messenger found their way to the camp, leaving me a small stack of letters from commanders and nobles demanding guidance, advice, or news to help calm their people. I hadn't even been crowned yet, and the responsibilities that were being heaped upon me were already becoming heavy. At least my mother and father had one another to help carry the burden of ruling a kingdom.

Messages were coming from all over asking for clarification on the political front, pleas for grain to be released to the southern marketplaces to keep troops from leaving their posts, and various calls for me to 'hurry up and take the bloody throne,' as one noble wrote. As if it were that simple. It took all of my patience to keep from writing scathing responses back to most of these fools. It appeared I was slowly cultivating enemies, and I hadn't even been given the chance to claim Freehaven as mine yet.

The longer I waited, the worse both rumors and public

opinion of me would become. Among the letters were reports from some of the military commanders stating that various hordes in the north had already heard of the kingdom's possible instability. Unless Freehaven unified again under a strong ruler, the hordes would attack us. We'd be weak if we didn't band together as a united people. Hidden among the letters was a statement from Skyhaven's commander, promising me the use of his keep and men should the need arise, and a warning about strange knights and worse roaming the countryside.

I wasn't sure if he just intended to scare me, but the small letter, which looked to have been hastily written, had caught my attention immediately. The death of my parents had set many things in motion. I would've sworn our group's smaller size would allow me to remain hidden from prying eyes, but it seemed people found me quicker than I'd thought possible. Had one of the noblemen leaked the privileged information?

I couldn't afford to spend time figuring out all the ways someone might have informed those after me about my whereabouts. Was a person among us helping those who meant me harm? There were just too many suspects, too many opportunities for someone sinister to listen in and report to whoever was behind all of this.

With a sigh, I thumbed through the documents again, arranging them into piles based on whether they needed my immediate attention or not. How did these blasted messengers keep finding me anyway? I understood how they'd found me after my parents had died. We weren't exactly hiding where we were. But very few people knew the path we'd taken home. I shook away the thought, dismissing it as I started working through the letters.

Tabitha soon came in with a few slices of cheese and

some bread to tide me over until the main meal was ready. She knew me well enough not to disturb my concentration.

By the time dinner was brought in, I knew why my father's expression had always soured when he heard that a messenger had arrived at court. It took a while to draft replies to those who needed immediate assistance, but when I was done, I gave them to Tabitha. She would deliver them to Sir Alan who could pass them off to the next messenger to visit camp.

Stretching back onto my bed, I pulled my sword from its sheath. The cold-looking blade had luckily never seen bloodshed before. It was light, but the hilt fit my hand well. As I turned the sword over in my hand, an unsettling feeling came over me. The blade would have its first taste of blood before this was all over.

6

EDWARD

At dusk, the travelers slowed near a large field. The servants and a few of the guards helped prepare the camp. Several of the knights had huddled around one man for a moment, before going their own ways. I laid low for a while, not wanting to risk alerting them to my presence. The large knight they'd been talking with already seemed on edge. I had noticed him watching his surroundings while on the road more than seemed necessary, as if he could sense me or someone else following the group.

I leaned against a thick tree on a hill near the camp, remaining sheltered from sight but able to hear what was going and sneak glances. The smell of their food twisted my stomach into knots, but I couldn't just waltz into their camp. They had a few guards who were patrolling the area where I was. It would probably be less risky for me to enter the camp when most of the knights were asleep.

Soft rain trickled down from the sky, growing heavier as the evening progressed. I shivered against the cold, but at least it deterred most of the men from lingering outside of their tents after supper. The guard patrol routes were heavier on the side of the encampment near the road rather than on the side near the woods where I sat. Their very important person must've been situated over there.

Weary and famished, I edged down the hill, making sure to stay under cover. The camp had begun quieting even more, so it might be time for me to make a move soon.

As I crept closer to the outskirts of camp, I heard a tree branch snap, closely followed by a young woman's giggle. Curiosity drove me forward, and I stepped carefully to not draw attention to myself. Her moan stopped me in my tracks. I scanned the trees, trying to locate the source of the sounds. About forty feet away, a guard and a servant girl embraced, oblivious to the world around them. Had it not been for her soft cries of passion, I might have walked into the pair. No wonder I'd not seen many guards at the back of camp. This must be some sort of lover's spot.

I circled the clearing a little away from them until I came upon their clothing. This might be the chance I was hoping for in order to better blend in with the camp. Among their possessions, I found a tunic and leather pants, along with a thick leather belt and a sheathed sword. That would be significantly more useful than my knife.

I carefully picked up the clothes and belt with its sheathed sword, careful to avoid any sound, then slunk away from the lovers. Why couldn't they have left a snack of some kind? It would've been so much easier than making my way through the camp. At least I had something less conspic-uous to wear now.

The guard's clothes smelled awful as I quickly changed into them. They could definitely use a wash. The leather belt hung low on my waist, but it would work so long as I didn't have to run any marathons. The patrol would be coming around any time now, and I wanted to be farther into the camp before then. They might decide to talk with me, and I needed to scope the area before I chose to interact with anyone.

A sleepy servant nodded to me as I passed him, and I let myself relax a little. The scent of cooked meat guided me toward where the food had been prepared.

Here and there, I ducked between the tents to avoid meeting anyone face to face. Twice I'd almost walked into guard patrols before I finally found my way to the camp's cooking tent. It was larger than the tents surrounding it, and none of the servants were around. They probably left for wherever they slept during the night. My focus narrowed on a small pile of bread that seemed to be left over from the evening's meal. I grabbed a few slices and folded them into what remained of my button-up shirt, using the formerly fine fabric as little more than a rag. A grimace formed on my lips, but I squelched it. When—if—I ever returned home, I had a closet full of clothes.

As I turned to leave, I spotted an array of salted meat laid out on one of the preparation tables. My stomach tightened with hunger. Bread was fine, but I needed protein after a full day of chasing this group on foot. I sliced off a piece and bit into it. My eyes watered as the heaps of salt they'd put on the meat overpowered all other flavor. The only thing I could tell from the meat was that this animal had been wild game. Made sense, especially if I'd been thrown back in time or some such. Nevertheless, the protein did wonders to invigorate me. I didn't feel quite so weak and drowsy now, but the small meal was a far cry from being completely sated. It was only a matter of time before someone came in here, and I didn't want to be found loitering. I preferred to keep my limbs attached.

I grabbed a couple more slices of meat, then made my way out of camp the way I'd come. Things settled down as more people began to rest for the night. In a matter of minutes, I was back in the shelter of the trees finishing off the meat and clearing my palate with a slice of bread. It was still warm from having been baked. It wasn't a thrilling meal, but seeing as I hadn't eaten properly for at least a day, I wasn't complaining.

The remaining two slices of bread sat on the remnants of the shirt in my lap. While I could eat them, I wasn't sure when I'd next be able to sneak food. It was only a matter of time before the guard noticed his clothes were missing and alerted the camp. I folded the slices of bread back into my shirt and trekked deeper into the woods. The hilltop where I'd rested before might be dangerous since it was near where the lovers had been, so I opted for climbing a tree once more to keep an eye on the camp.

Guards strolled along the camp making their rounds, but as my gaze scanned the area, I froze. For the briefest of moments, I spotted the outline of the woman from my dreams. There. She moved through the camp quietly, but I kept a keen eye on her. Even though I was some distance away, I couldn't shake the feeling building within me. It had to be the same woman. She had been scantily clad in the fields, but here she wore an elegant dress with a long cloak. She was the knights' VIP.

Puzzle pieces started clicking into place, but I couldn't take my eyes from her. Couldn't think rationally when she was right there.

Somewhere in the back of my head, I heard the feminine voice again beseeching me to help her. *She needs you. He'll kill her.* The middle-aged woman's voice echoed in my head over and over again. A protective instinct that I hadn't known I'd possessed stretched up from deep within me, but I pushed it down. Why should I be the one to guard her? She was in the middle of a military camp surrounded by well-armed men. I didn't know her, and she appeared to be perfectly fine.

My sleep was restless, and an uneasy weight rode my shoulders. Below me, a muffled cry in the shrubbery almost went unnoticed. Maybe it would have, if it hadn't been accompanied by the thud of a body hitting the tree I slept in. With a careful glance down, I caught a man in dark green strangling one of the guards. Blinking the sleep from my eyes, I looked out over the camp, and a chill slid down my spine. Men dressed in similar green tunics were systematically killing the knights. Key guards were going missing from their posts, and with morning light still another hour and a half or two hours away, few people in the camp were awake yet.

She. The thought pounded through my head, urging my body to act before I realized what was happening. *Needs.* I climbed down the tree. My heart pounded in my chest, heedless of what or who lay beneath me. *You.* The sword I'd acquired earlier sunk into the neck of the invader as I dropped on top of him. In a strangely detached state, I picked up my pace, leaving the weakened guard on the ground behind me. Tree roots and branches flew by my face as I sprinted through the woods. *Now!*

Whatever had risen up inside me had sparked a driving force to protect the young woman, but as I stood on the outskirts of camp, I froze as fear crashed through me. I'd lost sight of her during the climb down the tree. Would I be able to locate this woman from my dreams? A feminine scream cut through my fear, and I darted into the camp. Hesitation was a distant memory. Instead, I focused on picking my way through the clashing swords as knights began waking up and pushing back the group of invaders.

The invaders bore a mishmash of weapons and armor. They were merely hired thugs. The one thing they'd had on their side was the element of surprise. Two knights lay bleeding on the ground, and four of the mercenaries stood before a tent, which seemed to be the group's makeshift armory, as if they were guarding it.

Coming from the side of the tent, I slashed my sword through the nearest mercenary's side. My momentum carried me onward, and I smashed the pommel into the other merc's face. He clutched his nose, leaving himself wide open, and I slid the blade into his chest. It had happened in a matter of few heartbeats, but now I'd lost my own element of surprise. The last two spun toward me.

Quick and seemingly experienced with dirty fighting, the closest man swept my legs out from under me. The kick sent me face-first into the mud. Instead of coming to a stop, I rolled through the mud and leapt to my feet. His blade zinged through the air before it sank into the mud where my head had been moments ago. What I wouldn't give for more bullets. I needed to keep the ones I possessed for dire situations. This might not be fun, but it didn't fit my prerequisites for dire. The knights had risen to their feet during the fight and saw their chance to push back the mercenaries.

I backed away from the melee and headed farther into the camp. The woman was nowhere to be found. My head ached as tension squeezed my temples.

Before me was a tent larger and grander than the rest. The sound of sword clashing against sword came from within, and I slashed my way through the tent's fabric. Two heavily armored mercenaries stood before the lady I'd seen in the fields. One of the men wielded a large club, while the other carried a longsword crimson with blood. The woman was bent over a little with one hand pressed against her side, her other held a sword with just a hint of blood on it. She was definitely in over her head.

Everyone's gaze turned to me at once. The woman's eyebrows came together, and she opened her mouth as if to speak, then stopped. For a few moments, we all just stared at one another before the oaf wielding the club shoved the woman through an opening they must've cut into the tent.

My last glimpse of the young woman was her feebly trying to stab her abductor, but he easily used his club to knock the sword from her hand. She cried out in pain, then they were out of sight.

The mercs' mission was pretty clear: while the rest of the group slaughtered and distracted the guards, these two were here to kidnap the woman. They would pay dearly for that choice.

The remaining mercenary stalked forward. He gripped his longsword with two hands and placed his right foot forward, tilting the sword slightly to the left. For the first time in a while, I was grateful to my mother for enrolling me in those fencing classes. They might not be incredibly helpful against a professional swordsman, but I had a better chance of surviving the night with the knowledge I'd gained from them.

I kept an eye on his form and feinted to the left. The moment my foot rose from the ground, he moved. He was quick, almost too quick for me. Instead of ducking out of the way of his strike, I lifted my sword and let his momentum push him onto my blade. His eyes widened, and the soft clatter of metal rang out in the tent as his longsword fell from his grip. I jerked my sword from his gut, and he tumbled backward, disbelief in his eyes. Blood seeped from his stomach, staining his leather armor. The man was still alive, but his eyes showed signs of defeat. He'd be dead within a matter of minutes.

I rushed from the tent where the female had been taken. A little way off, the abductor was trying without success to get the young woman onto the back of a horse. He shook his club at her and swung it as if he'd knock her out, but he didn't. That was just as telling. Either he didn't want to injure her, or the person he worked for had ordered her to be taken unharmed. From the blood coating her hand, I bet the man wouldn't be looked upon highly if he returned, and I needed to make sure he didn't.

The man's sheer size was intimidating, and I wasn't sure how long I'd be able to handle him in combat. Not with that ridiculous club.

Bloody hell.

This situation was looking more and more dire. I pulled my gun from the hem of my leather pants and released the safety. The merc turned his head in my direction as he climbed into the saddle, throwing the woman in front of him on her belly, and howled in rage. Maybe the other bloke had meant something to him. Great. Now he'd drawn more attention to us. Taking a few deep breaths, I waited for the perfect shot between his eyes. It wasn't as if he could fire back.

At seven feet away, I released a breath and squeezed the trigger. Simple target practice. Part of me felt sorry for the man. He'd have no idea what hit him. The big man sat up straighter and lifted his club, then he jerked back as the bullet hit him. It was off-target, but it'd still be lethal. He tumbled from the horse, nearly taking the woman with him, but she clung to the saddle as the animal reared back and came to a sudden stop.

The tall knight I recognized from the road walked out of the tent behind me, and I tucked my gun out of sight. He glanced between me and the big man, his sword aimed warily at us. The kidnapper turned his head, showing off the wound in his throat before he clamped his hands to it, trying in vain to keep his blood inside of him.

Ignoring the two of them, I jogged toward the horse to check on the woman. Her grip slipped on the saddle just as I reached her, and she slid toward the ground. I caught her in my arms and cradled her to my chest.

"It's going to be okay. You're safe," I said in calming tones. I'd had plenty of experience with placating others in my line of work. Now that she was safe, a strange relief welled within my chest.

She blinked up at me, giving me the first good look at her face. Her beauty was even more alluring than I'd imagined. I wasn't usually swept up by the fairer sex like this, but something about her enticed me, even though I knew it shouldn't. She grimaced in pain, and I looked down toward her abdomen.

"May I see your wound?"

"Yo-you saved me. Tha-thank you, sir." Her voice was thready, and she was cool to the touch. She was going into shock. I needed to get her somewhere safe where I could inspect her wound. There was still fighting around us, but it seemed like the full force of the knights were gaining the upper hand against the mercenaries. "Are you a doctor?"

"It's not a problem. And no, I'm not a doctor, but I've learned a thing or two when it comes to wounds on the battlefield." I lowered my hand to her side to try to gain access to the wound.

The tall knight thrust his sword at me before I could do much, pressing the tip against my chest hard enough that I felt a pinch of pain. "Unhand the princess of Freehaven, or I'll take your arm. She deserves your respect, soldier. She doesn't need your help. I shall have the camp's doctor brought to her at once."

I looked between them. "Princess? Are you kidding...?" My voice trailed off when I met her gaze. "She shouldn't be moved far. She needs a few warm blankets and to have her wound looked at immediately." I stared back at the knight. "I can help her. You have to trust me, for her sake."

7

BRIGIT

My savior had stayed by my side doing what he could for the wound until the camp's doctor came. Sir Alan had him taken away then, perhaps a little more forcibly than necessary.

Something about the man was strange. He wore the clothes of a guard, but he didn't appear to be from the area, either in physical appearance or in accent...and then there was that loud bang that had happened shortly before my kidnapper fell off the horse. How had he been able to attack from that range without a bow and arrows? *It has to be magic.* Honestly, though, I didn't care. What mattered was that he'd saved my life.

"Sir Alan, please bring me the man who rescued me. I have a few questions for him." I propped myself up on the soft pillows covering my straw mattress, so I wouldn't appear indisposed when I saw him again. I didn't even know his name, but something about him stoked my curiosity.

When Sir Alan returned with the man, he guided him to the table on the far side of my tent. Rope bound his wrists, and the man kept glaring at Sir Alan who stood between us, as if concerned the man would suddenly attack.

I wanted to shake my head in frustration, but we still didn't know much about him. Maybe he'd shown up to make himself look like a hero. Could he have been part of the attack? I didn't want to believe he was. He'd risked his life for me.

"What is your name?" I asked him.

"Edward Emerson, and yours?" His tone was bland, and the frown on his face deepened as Sir Alan started to draw his sword. I knew the tirade he'd launch into. Did this Edward truly not know who I was? That hadn't happened often in my life. He didn't uphold the pretenses many others clung to when they spoke to me.

"Put away your sword, Sir Alan." I held my hand up. "My name is Brigit Ó Ruaidh, Princess of Freehaven. It's a pleasure to meet you."

"Yes, Your Highness." Sir Alan slid the sword back into its sheath. "It would be wise to greet the princess in a manner befitting her station," he growled at Edward.

"Forgive me, Your Highness," Edward said. He looked between us but didn't say anything else.

"Where do you come from? Sir Alan doesn't know you, so I don't think you're actually a guard here. Besides, I've never heard that accent before." I started to reposition myself, but stopped as pain clenched my side. The memory of Edward's tender touch on my skin as he inspected the wound came back to me, and heat caressed my cheeks. Now wasn't the time to think like that. He might be attractive, but I still wasn't sure if I should trust him, considering that someone tried to kidnap me not long ago.

"I'm not from here." He regarded me with an intense

stare that put me a little on edge. His gaze slid lower when I moved, and then he met my eyes again.

"I know. That's what I just said." I sighed, and it took all my dignity not to clench my hands into fists and rest my head against the pillow. It probably would've hurt quite a bit, and I'd end up looking like a petulant child who hadn't gotten her way. My reputation was already in tatters. When we were alone again, Sir Alan would surely scold me for letting myself be injured. "Please, answer the question."

"London, England."

Geography had always been one of my favorite subjects as a child, but I'd never heard of any such location. "London?" I exchanged a glance with Sir Alan who shrugged. So I wasn't crazy. "Where is that?"

"I came through a large door with a skeleton key lock, which disappeared when I got here." He shook his head, disgust plain on his face. "Your name sounds Irish, so I'm surprised you haven't heard of England. But maybe you lot are in some alternate past. I don't know."

A skeleton key and a disappearing door? A chill ran up my spine, and I leveled a hard stare at Edward. "Do you know what you're saying? If you're telling the truth, then you traveled here from another realm. Those doors appear to very few people. The people of my kingdom supposedly journeyed through one to Freehaven from the Emerald Isles in another realm we call the Gauntlet..."

He narrowed his eyes at me and leaned forward. "The Emerald Isles? That's Ireland. I'm pretty sure your people came from my realm. Do you know where to find these doors?"

Sir Alan smacked his fist on the table in front of Edward, making Edward lean back a little. He shot a glare at my knight that might have made others shrink away. "You're not in a position to ask questions of the princess. You're in my custody here, if you didn't notice."

"If *you* didn't notice, I saved her life. Where were you when she was being dragged onto the back of a horse and almost carried away?" He moved his arms as if to cross them over his chest, but they were still bound so he placed his hands in his lap.

Sir Alan raised his arm as if to backhand Edward. "You'll regret that arrogant attitude, boy."

"Stop it! Now." I pushed to my feet and pressed a hand gently against my side, pushing down the incredible pain. If I needed to break up their fight myself, I would. Something about Edward attracted me to him. I couldn't help it. But I refused to endure their bickering. "Do not take him far, Sir Alan, and if he's hurt when I next see him, we shall be having words." I waved them away with a flick of my wrist and started to sink back into bed when another thought occurred to me. "Wait."

The two men stared at me. Neither of them had moved yet.

"How did you injure my abductor? You were at a distance from him."

"I shot him with a gun, Your Highness. My people have more advanced technology than yours. I knew if I didn't shoot him, he would take you away, and I hoped to prevent that. The ammunition for my weapon is limited, so I only used it because I felt it was absolutely necessary." He rose to his feet and looked at the knight. "We should let her rest."

"I'd like a report in a few hours, Sir Alan, on the troops and how the camp fared during the attack."

He bowed his head toward me, then shoved Edward out of the tent.

As they left, Tabitha walked in, carrying an herbal paste

to rub across my bruises where the larger man had grabbed at me. I breathed a sigh of relief and gave her a small smile. "I'm glad you're here. Those men were starting to infuriate me."

At least dealing with bruises didn't involve a doctor. Tabitha was well able to take care of them. As she applied the paste, I thought back on my parents. How would I be able to take care of Freehaven if I had to keep one eye over my shoulder? The constant fear of who would attack me next might drive me insane.

"What do you think of him, Your Highness?" Tabitha asked as she laid a bandage over the paste to keep it from rubbing off.

"Who?" I asked, looking away from her. From the intensity of her stare, I could only guess. "He seems different, maybe dangerous. It's difficult to know who we can trust. His sudden appearance was either planned or magical. I'm not sure which would make me feel less anxious." Even as I spoke of him, thoughts of his strong jawline and piercing blue eyes came to mind.

"It would be a shame if something were to happen to him before we found out," Tabitha noted. "He saved your life. It'd likely be wise to keep him close. If he's one of our enemies, we can leverage him. If he's not, he would be too good an ally to lose." Her voice was more soothing than the bandages on my wounds. She gave wise advice.

I readjusted my dress back into place. "Could you do me a favor, Tabitha? Please check to make sure he's okay. I trust Sir Alan, but I'm uncomfortable with the idea that they might be roughing him up. He appears to have talents we might need in the future. He saved me once, so maybe he'd be willing to side with us against whoever is after me." Hope crept into my voice before I could stop it.

With a deep bow of her head, Tabitha rose to her feet, then retreated from the tent.

My parents had never shown discomfort while walking among the masses wherever the crown required them. Neither had they shown fear or concern about being assassinated at any given moment. I longed to have the strength they did. The least I could do was take their guidance to heart and press on.

Whoever was behind all this would suffer. I wasn't blinded by fury or rage. I simply promised myself that the culprits would find themselves in a most unbearable position, and I'd watch them slowly perish. Not because of hate, but I had to know justice had been served.

I ambled around the tent, taking a few practice swings with my sword to reacclimate to its use. I'd failed when faced with the two attackers. My lessons had slipped away as fear took over.

Ten minutes of practicing different strikes and feints built back a little self-esteem. I knew how to use the sword. I just needed to put my training into practice when it mattered.

"Your Highness," Sir Alan called with a tap against the leather covering the tent.

"Come in."

The soft sound of the flaps moving aside drew my attention as he made his way inside the tent. He bowed his head with a thoughtful look on his face, as if he were trying to find the right words. The few times he'd acted this way in the past, it was because he knew what he was going to say might upset me. Was this the scolding I'd feared?

"Please, Sir Alan, say what you need to say."

"Well, there are two options with our 'guest.' Either way, we are in his debt. He saved you, regardless of his possible motives. He might be a spy, but that makes little sense because he prevented you from being taken. Unless there is a third party after you as well. The second option makes me more uneasy." He cleared his throat and shifted his feet. "I'm concerned that he is telling the truth, and you were saved by a stroke of luck," he said. "We failed you. There is no way around it. I should've suspected an attack, and even so I wasn't able to reach you in time. If he hadn't been there, we would have lost you."

In all the times I'd known Sir Alan, I'd never seen him emotionally distressed before. "You've served my family loyally all these years. I have faith in you that it won't happen again." I said, keeping my eyes locked with his.

There was a momentary pause before he unsheathed his sword and placed it on the table between us. "I may not be up for the task. I fear I alone can't guarantee your safety. We need to reconsider progressing toward Freehaven's capital." He kept his hand on his sword's pommel, stroking it with his thumb. "I hate to suggest it, but the kingdom can't lose you. If we do, it'll all be pointless anyway." Shaking his head, he released his sword.

"What are you saying, Sir Alan? I need to claim the throne. The kingdom needs its rightful ruler. I know you're afraid of losing me, but I can't let fear stand in the way of taking my place among my people. Besides, with you at my side, who would dare to oppose me?" I smiled at him.

"You are the last of your father's line. Without you, the kingdom will descend into infighting and possibly tyranny. That is how kingdoms and empires fall. That is how your ancestors were able to carve out this land for themselves generations ago. The people need you to rule, yes. But they need you alive to do that," Sir Alan stated. Fire burned in his eyes, and I could feel the depth of emotion behind them. He truly would do anything to keep me safe.

"A tyrant claiming the throne for even a year might mean he'll have gathered an army, possibly by drafting my own peasants. I refuse to fight against the very people I've been destined to keep safe. It goes against everything my father ever drilled into me. Excuse me, Sir Alan, but we are both tired. Take up your sword and rest for now." I kept my voice steady, not wanting this discussion to continue any longer.

His lips quirked a little, showing the barest hint a smile. "As you wish, princess." He retrieved his sword and left.

8

EDWARD

I sat on the ground, waiting for my captors to decide my fate. My hands were tied to the tent's sturdy support pole behind me. From what I'd heard, there was a power play going on in this kingdom. The reaction to my gun even further emphasized that wherever the bloody hell I was seemed to have a medieval level of technology.

Still, I'd saved the princess of a kingdom I had few details on, made friends and enemies I had no context for, and followed a dreamlike notion that this woman was my anchor. Mine to protect.

It sounded silly, because I was an assassin—someone who solved others' problems in the shadows, when everything else had failed. I'd just done the opposite. This wasn't a mission. I'd merely obeyed the voices in my head to help a woman I'd dreamed about.

Those who killed wantonly became my targets. I made sure they got what they deserved. I knew every one of them and could easily give reasons why the world was a better place without them. Some were common criminals, while others were infamous worldwide, but every one of their deaths was justifiable and authorized. I didn't save people. I merely took the lives of those who caused pain and misery.

Saving people was a different animal. The princess might be safe for the time being, but in the long run, she'd likely need to be rescued again.

I shook my head. I was sure they didn't want my help even if I offered it. Besides, I was an assassin, not a defender. Staying a few steps ahead of other assassins in this world would not be easy. I had no intel or satellites to give me an advantage. Then again, the people after her had no idea who I was either.

Should I lure the assassin in by using her as bait, or should I keep her sheltered from harm? Were the assassins enemies or just deluded mercenaries? I didn't have enough details to make a solid decision, and I hated operating from an emotional standpoint alone.

Sir Alan followed the princess's command with a level head and didn't seem too quick to jump to conclusions. Her subjects appeared to follow her out of respect, not fear. The chances of her being a tyrant were slim.

But I really didn't belong here. My firearm, my way of thinking, and the skills I possessed didn't mesh with this world. If these people knew of a way for me to return to my world, I'd take it in a heartbeat. After all, my life wasn't here.

My thoughts returned to my world, where I'd witnessed horrible things done in the name of revenge, faith, and all sorts of other justifications. But there was also good. England, despite its problems, was my home. I'd served the Crown without question. It held a fond place in my heart, and it always would. I had responsibilities not many could handle. Poor Croft would lose his mind going over the wreckage, trying to figure out what happened to me. I just hoped that whoever else had been in the building had escaped.

Pushing to my feet, I rolled my neck to try to release the tension there. I didn't know what I was going to do or even what I wanted here. It seemed the princess wasn't a tyrant, and if anything, she needed all the help she could muster in order to stabilize the kingdom we were in.

A woman walked into the tent and looked me over. She was carrying what appeared to be herbs and other supplies in a basket, but I could make out the outline of a concealed dagger, barely hidden beneath her fabric belt.

I slid my back down the pole and crouched there, keeping her in the field of my vision. If she were to lash out, I'd be prepared. "What's your name, miss?" I asked as she walked closer.

"Tabitha. Don't do anything you might regret, stranger. There are knights outside," she said softly.

I nodded to the pole behind me. "I don't think you have to worry about that." I kept my gaze on her. When she didn't say anything else, I told my name and just waited.

After a few moments, she reached for something in her basket, which it almost made me jump to attention. "Don't rush with the basket. I'm aware of the knife you're trying to hide. While I doubt you've been sent here to kill me, I still don't know who to trust," I said, keeping my voice low to prevent any nearby guards from listening in.

Tabitha gave me a soft smile. "Maybe there is more to you than meets the eye." She gave me an appraising look. "Has anyone hurt you? Some of the mercenaries had poisoned blades, and Sir Alan wanted me to ensure you didn't die before they decided your fate." Her voice increased in pitch in a few places, and she was blinking more than when she first entered the tent.

The telltale signs of her lies mattered little to me. I didn't care who'd sent her. I was more interested in why she'd seen the need to lie. "Lies don't suit you, Tabitha." I sighed. "No, they didn't cut me. I merely sustained a few bruises. I've been through worse." I gave a brief rundown on my encounter with the men in the princess's tent.

Tabitha's eyes were still wide from me noticing her lie. When she finally collected herself, she grabbed her basket and started to leave, then stopped. "If your story is true, why did you care about what would happen to her?"

"I'm not sure. Before I woke up here, I saw her in a dream. There were green fields and thunder rumbling in the distance. She needed my help." I spoke truthfully, but a few details I wanted to keep private—like the princess's nearly naked form in my vision.

Her mouth opened slightly as a slight blush filled her cheeks. The first wave of giggles left her lips before I could ask her not to laugh. It took a few moments for her to realize I was being honest. "What? Are you sure? I thought that only happened in bardic tales." Her smile melted into a frown.

"Trust me. It sounds like some sort of bizarre fantasy novel, but here I am. What can you tell me about the princess?"

For a few heartbeats, she hesitated. Her brow creased, then she shook her head. "I'm really not at liberty to tell you anything. My apologies." With that, she collected her things and left.

"Shite. I meant no harm." I knew she wanted the best for her princess, but I was merely curious to know more about the woman I'd saved.

I sat on the ground and leaned my head back against the pole. I'd been meaning to catch up on sleep. Now was my chance. It seemed I'd be here for a while.

9

BRIGIT

Sir Alan had been gone a while by the time Tabitha returned. My mind still raced, going back over our conversation and the fact that he'd laid down his sword. I hated that Sir Alan felt helpless to protect me. I also mulled over the next day's schedule. We couldn't afford any more incidents like this along the road.

While Skyhaven was close, the surrounding woods were great ambush locations for a group of travelers who didn't pay attention. So far we hadn't been ambushed on the move, but that could change. Being on horseback was advantageous, but a few assassins with crossbows could do serious harm to the brave knights.

"Did you learn anything interesting?" I asked Tabitha as she sat at the table. She had a way about her that could make most men turn their heads, but few paid attention to the knife she kept hidden under her belt. She'd moved the knife, which was concerning. "Did you have to use your weapon?"

"Your Highness, Edward is more interesting than I'd

originally thought. He has brains, but there's something more hidden just beneath the surface." She sighed. "To answer your other question, no. I moved the knife after he spotted it. He has keen eyes and good intuition, more than I'd imagine a mercenary would possess."

"Can we trust him?" He'd saved my life, and even though he'd had a chance to kill or kidnap me, he'd checked to make sure I was safe.

"I believe so, but I would keep an eye on him." She shook her head and stood. "You're vulnerable. There will likely be those who want to take advantage of that. I didn't get that feeling from him, but one never knows."

"Of course. I'm going to see him." I walked toward the tent's entrance, and Tabitha followed after me. I held up my hand to ward her off. "I'll go alone." Why did everyone think I didn't need space to breathe?

"As you wish, Your Highness." Tabitha bowed her head.

As I made my way through the camp, I saw the on-duty guards had been doubled again. Sir Alan wasn't taking any chances with mercenaries invading the camp again. An extra knight was even stationed at the entrance to Edward's tent. He seemed more tense than usual. Sir Alan had likely torn into everyone over how they'd let down their guard.

"Your Highness." Sir Orlan, one of my father's knights, bowed to me and pulled back the tent flap. "If he gives you any trouble, we'll be right here. Just call for assistance."

"I will, sir. Thank you." My reply sounded hollow in my ears as I pushed ahead to question Edward. He was tied to a pole in the center of the tent with his legs stretched out before him. From the sound of it, he was fast asleep.

Conscious of what Tabitha had told me, I didn't trust his posture. Instead, I stood some space away from him and waited.

After a few moments, he finally lifted his chin up a little. "Your Highness," Edward said, sleep roughing his voice.

"Are you well?" The question was out of my mouth before I could hold it back. I was confident Tabitha and Sir Alan had taken care of him, aside from tying him to the pole.

"I'm fine. But I hardly think that's why you're here." Edward rolled his neck as if to loosen building tension there. Something about his graceful movements drew my attention, scrambling my thoughts at times.

"Yes, you're right. I want to trust you, but I have enemies who want me dead. My parents were assassinated, and I'm afraid without your intervention, I would have been next." I paced my side of the tent, feeling anxiety tighten my chest. "My family has ruled this kingdom for generations. Now I'm in a position where I don't know who to trust." I caught myself halfway through and turned the discussion to focus on him. "I know we talked earlier, but I need to ask you this directly. Are you an assassin?"

The slightest smile twisted Edward's lips. "To be honest, yes, but don't worry, you are not one of my marks. In my world, I worked for my queen. My sole dedication was to ensure the people's safety. Some people considered themselves above the law's reach. In those rare occasions, I was employed under strict rules. Each of my targets was dangerous to those around them, with no regard for who they hurt in pursuit of their goals." As he spoke, his eyes became distant, focusing on something only he could see.

"I guess I'll have to take your word for it." Oddly enough, it didn't surprise me that he was an assassin, but I was quite intrigued that he worked for his queen.

"I'm not a knight. I do what needs to be done. You will need to trust me as there's no one here to vouch for me or regale you with my past heroics. But that's not really needed here, is it? You have assassins after you, and I was trained as one. We may have different weapon skills and techniques, but our natural inclinations unite us." He paused for a moment, then met my gaze. "How do I leave your realm?"

"I'm not sure, but don't lose hope quite yet. The library at my family's castle has an extensive collection of the lore and history of this world. If there is a record of these doors, we will find it there. You are welcome to any information on the subject within it. You saved my life after all."

Edward's eyes narrowed when I mentioned the library. "If I ensure your safety, you mean? I'm lousy at protecting people, but as an assassin, my skills haven't found their match yet." His demeanor seemed to shift at the thought of going home. He was more focused.

He'd already kept me safe once, and if his words were true, he'd be invaluable in rooting out other assassins and preventing more attempts on my life. He had plenty of incentive to keep me alive.

"I don't have many allies here, and the ones I do have might be traitors to my cause. Your proposal is acceptable, Edward. Do you then pledge your service to me?" I asked him directly. I had a feeling any vows might be lost on him.

"Yes, Your Highness, I pledge to keep you safe." He bowed his head to me. There was something more to the moment than I could put my finger on, but I was honestly just glad he was on my side. The more allies I had, the better, particularly if I was to reclaim my throne.

A commotion outside drew my attention.

After a moment, Sir Alan barged into the tent with Sir Orlan in tow. "You let her in here without guards? Are you insane?" he yelled.

Sir Orlan glanced around the room, as if checking for anything out of place. "See for yourself, Sir Alan. She is alive and unharmed. He is still tied to the column and unable to move around. You have nothing to worry about."

"Sirs, I'm fine. What is going on?" I turned my gaze to my old teacher. This was unlike him. It took me a moment to realize there were new dents in his armor that I hadn't noticed earlier. My thoughts ran wild with speculation. Were we under attack again? He'd doubled the guards, yet now his armor was dented. It didn't make sense.

"Forgive me, Your Highness. I had a heated argument with some of our fellow knights. It's nothing for you to worry about." He glared at Sir Orlan who'd begun to open his mouth. Neither of the two knights spoke for a few minutes as they glared at one another.

"Both of you are terrible liars. How many knights tried to defect?" Edward said as he rose to his feet. He brought his hands out from behind his back. They were bright red and a little bloody. How...? Tension built in the air until I feared they'd start fighting again. I had to intervene.

"Sirs, Edward, stop it. Sir Orlan, what were you going to say?" I kept my words terse, letting my agitation bleed into my voice. They would tell me the truth whether they liked it or not. I couldn't have anyone keeping things from me, not now.

"Two guards tried to flee. Both were young men who'd only been with us a few months. Sir Alan found them and tried to convince them to return. When that failed, he had to take matters into his own hands. We can't allow deserters to wander into nearby towns and run their mouths to anyone who will listen after a few pints of ale." Sir Orlan kept his voice steady and his gaze on Sir Alan. "He didn't want to tell you because he knew you'd be concerned. This happens from time to time. New, untested men become afraid and try to leave. You love your people, but your safety comes first."

Deserters, great. Not what I needed to hear right now.

10

EDWARD

The tension in the tent had lessened after the truth came to light about the deserters and Sir Alan's actions. I wasn't sure how Brigit would take the news. Her attention remained locked on Sir Alan, as if she were trying to decide what to do.

"Did you know them?" she asked, a hint of sorrow dampening her voice.

Sir Orlan started to speak, but Sir Alan lifted his hand to quiet him. "It's all right, Sir Orlan. Yes, Your Highness, I knew them. Two sons of a farmer who lives not far from here. Both were squires, and seemed loyal, but apparently neither of them had the grit to risk their lives for their princess. I took no pleasure in ending their lives. It just had to be done." His voice was calm.

The atmosphere had become solemn. Those kids had taken too much on themselves and deserted. Their mistake was doing it in a time when their kingdom was unstable. My own memories of serving my country returned for a few moments. "It can happen to anyone. Trainees, those prepared, or those experienced in the field. None of it matters when things get tough and everything seems to go wrong. It's easy to be a soldier during times of peace, but men don't know who they are until they meet their own limits. Just because they met their limits is no reflection on you, sir. You did your duty. There is no shame or dishonor in that. Your Highness, may I speak with you alone?" My own voice regained some of the authority I'd used when commanding a squad before leaving military service behind.

For the first time, Sir Alan looked at me with more than disdain in his eyes. He appeared to recognize a fellow warrior in me. With a brief nod, he excused himself and left the tent. If I had to trust one man in this camp besides myself, it would be him. Someone who could kill without remorse had little humanity left in them. The fact he cared about the two he killed spoke much of his character.

As Sir Orlan left, I walked toward the back of the tent to pace. Being tied to the pole had been restrictive, and I needed to stretch and move around to get the circulation going again in my legs.

"Sir Alan did what he had to, and he feels horrible about it. That's the sign of a good man. But I get the feeling there's more going on between you two than a knight and his princess," I said without really expecting an answer.

"Sir Alan was my tutor from a young age. He served with my father. When my father and mother went away on trips to keep the kingdom running smoothly, he put Sir Alan in charge of looking after me. His patience has made him a great politician and fighter. It didn't take long for us to grow close. He's a wonderful man who swore to ensure the safety of the throne. He has declined many offers of marriage to avoid being distracted from his primary task. In short, he's the most loyal knight a princess can hope to have."

"I find it hard to believe such an imposing man was your tutor. He would have been twice your size. Did he teach you history while clad in armor?" I tried out a bit of humor to clear the air.

"Goodness, no. I had other teachers too. He primarily taught me sword fighting and strategy. For a time, I thought my parents might be considering a marriage between us, but it wasn't to be." Relief filled her expression. "However, life in court showed me the darker side of people, and the pettiness most nobles seem to harbor. I dreaded that my parents would arrange a political marriage between me and some portly baron who cared more about himself than cultivating love. My mother and father always had a caring and warm relationship, which really meant something to me. With most arranged marriages, there isn't any warmth, kindness or real love. My parents had that, though, and I hoped one day I'll have that too. But Sir Alan is quite married to his position." A soft smile played upon her lips. It felt good seeing her mood lift.

"He is dedicated, even for a knight. I was in a similar situation to his. I didn't make any commitments or spend time on anything other than my work. The moments when I might have been able to, it seemed the dread of something bad happening to them killed my chances. It was easier to just live for my work. I guess I never thought about finding the right person to spend the rest of my life with. People in my profession rarely do, anyway. There's a lot of danger involved. It wouldn't be a good life for either of us." I'd never really opened up to anyone about my life. What was it about Brigit that made it easy? "What strikes me as almost comical is that growing up I was always told I'd be a heartbreaker, but the only heart I've ever broken was my own." I completed my train of thought and looked at the tent flaps leading outside.

"It's a shame. Do you need anything else tonight?" The softness of her voice had thrown me completely off my game. I'd enjoyed her company so much I nearly missed the quiet movements at the front of the tent.

I raised a finger to my lips and turned toward the entrance. Anyone could cut holes into a tent, but that would be noisy with the fabric tearing. If an intruder could use the tent's entrance to avoid attention, they would. With a few quick steps, I closed the distance to the entrance and pulled the flap aside. I held my knife at my side in case it was a merc. When I caught Tabitha's outline against the torchlight outside, I came to a stop. Brigit and I must've been in the tent longer than I'd thought.

"Come in. Don't skulk about." I waved Tabitha into the tent. She hesitated a moment before walking in, giving her princess a slightly questioning look that lasted a few moments before she dipped into a curtsy.

I took the opportunity to stare past the guards toward the partly cloudy sky above. The fresh scent of rain was in the air, strong enough to break through the usual assortment of camp scents. The wind had picked up, and storms brewed in the distance.

Remembering my dream, I stole a glance back inside the tent to ensure Brigit was safe and secure. Whatever the dream had been about, it led me here. And there had been violent storms nearby, dangerous storms.

Whatever the reason, be it destiny, coincidence, or something more, I didn't care. Being close to her made me feel it was worth leaving my life on hold. My job in London could wait.

This was a whole new world. I had someone to protect, and I'd do that until I'd reached the castle's library. When we reached that point, I'd see what my choices were.

11

BRIGIT

The journey from our camp to Skyhaven Keep had taken longer than expected. With the assault, we had left later in the day than we'd have liked, which went on to require another night of camp farther down the road.

But at last, we were here. I still remembered when my parents brought me to the keep the first time. I'd felt so far away from home that I'd asked my father if we were in another kingdom. The memory of his laughter and the loving smile he'd shared with my mother faded back into the depths of my mind.

This time, my trek here wasn't quite as innocent.

Someone wanted to kill me and take what was rightfully mine. On the last stretch of road, Sir Alan forced a group of peasants and smaller merchants off the road due to the risk that one of them might be an assassin. It was not the impression I wanted to make with my people—some pompous noble shoving the poor aside on the way to her big house.

Skyhaven's big gates and extended overlook towers were

designed to withstand most sieges. It would be a safe stop on my trip home. As we entered, the local guardsmen, who were all loyal to my father when he'd still been alive, came to assist us. No lord or a noble currently oversaw the keep, which made it even more valuable. The soldiers stationed here cared little about politics, and their commander had a reputation for being a strict and honest man.

The keep served several functions: it was a central station for local guardsmen, a strong military checkpoint between the castle and main trade routes, and it also ensured no forbidden goods were allowed in the cities along the road. Despite the trade traffic in the lower courtyard, the keep proper was secure, and very few non-military personnel were allowed inside. Anyone caught sneaking around in its halls would soon find themselves in the dungeons below.

I followed Sir Alan through the secondary gates and into the inner courtyard. Knights surrounded us, and I tried to focus on breathing. I couldn't afford to let my guard down. The other night's attack still shook me to the core, but I balled my hand into a fist to keep it from moving to the hilt of my sword.

Skyhaven's commander was fairly friendly. His face had deep scars earned during battles throughout his life. A twinkle of happiness lit his eyes as he spotted me. Sir Alan and the commander exchanged a few quiet words before I was lead further into the keep. We took a tight set of stairs up to the commander's quarters.

I released a nervous sigh. Maybe this would turn out just fine after all. Across the hall from the commander's quarters was the keep's main office. It was held aside for any member of the royal family and would function as my room while we stayed here.

The main office had a fantastic view over the other towers and the huge metal drawbridge door. It was meant for royalty, and it showed. Heavy, expensive benches and cloth-lined chairs were placed near the walls, giving anyone visiting the room a comfortable seating arrangement regardless of their status. I was more than ready to sit down after those stairs, but Edward barred my entry into the room.

"No, this won't do," he said and turned to leave, blocking my way.

Sir Alan grabbed him on the elbow. "What do you mean?"

Edward sighed and pointed to the opened windows and the breathtaking view beyond. "If she's here, her location is easy to find. Someone could see her at the window and shoot her with an arrow. If they don't know where she is, they can't attack her. It only takes one keen-eyed civ...peasant to see that the princess is in this tower. No, it's not safe. If I intend to protect her, this room will not do," he said.

Anger boiled up inside of me, but I calmed myself. He'd said he was trained as an assassin. If he thought this wouldn't work, then I should listen. He'd already saved me once. "I see your point. Is there another room here that would work better?"

We checked half a dozen rooms before Edward seemed content on one in the middle of the tower. It had no windows. Instead, heavy bookshelves lined the walls. My hopes for the royal family's room sank. This room seemed to fit what he wanted.

Even so, he ventured around the shelves, perhaps testing for secret passages, until he was satisfied. With another glance at the door to gauge its thickness, he finally nodded. "This is the best so far," he said and nodded toward Sir

Alan. "It's nicely isolated with no visibility. Thick walls and the door seems solid enough. This will do." He glanced in my direction as if watching my reaction.

The thought of being locked up in a windowless room surrounded by books as opposed to a nice view wasn't a pleasant one. But in the light of the assassination attempt, I'd have to choose safety over vanity any day. I nodded my approval.

Sir Alan spoke quietly to one of the knights he'd brought with him who then took off. "We'll make sure the door is well-guarded, Your Highness."

"Thank you, sir."

My gaze locked with Edward's as everyone else vacated the room. Something about him drew me in. Something that felt real, if not magical. I wondered if he felt the same way, or if I was just off-balance after the recent attack.

He finally turned to the books around the room. "Could anything in here be useful to help us narrow down our list of suspects?" he asked as he browsed the spines on the nearest volumes.

The books my parents liked to keep in each study had a collection of volumes on terrain, maps, and genealogical information on the noble families. I scanned the shelves until I found a book on my royal bloodline and any other important tomes I could think of. Meanwhile, Edward had located a set of maps along the wall and was studying them intently. He trailed his finger over their surfaces as if soaking up the information and creating his own mental map of the kingdom.

I walked around the desk and arranged the entire situation in my head. I was still some ways off from reaching the capital and claiming the throne. From my family, there were really only five people who could contest my right to rule.

Each of their lineages came through the royal bloodline via my great-grandfather. None had shown magical talent, as was expected of rulers, but I'd felt power burn inside me before as if I carried my own untapped magic. No one needed to know that.

"Do you have any enemies who could claim the right to rule by conquest?" Edward kept his voice low as he sauntered over to the desk and looked over the book on my family's lineage.

"No. Neither my parents nor I had enemies...until now. Whoever is after the throne is likely from my family. The people of my kingdom would rise up against an outsider. My parents and I weren't close with parts of my family. Some served in active roles of government under my parents, but a few disliked us. None of them should have a reason to have them killed, though." I sat in the cushioned chair before my legs gave out.

Edward lifted my chin and brushed his thumb over my cheek. "Don't worry. We'll sort this out." He smiled. "Let's try another angle. Who were your parents not close to? Who would have a claim and the drive to accomplish something like this?"

"A couple of cousins, an aunt, and an uncle."

"It should be someone with a desire to carve themselves a path they wouldn't otherwise get without violence." Edward dipped the quill in ink and scribbled on the parchment before us. "Tell me what you know of each."

It took a few hours of talking about my family's internal politics, what they'd say about each other, and rumors associated with them. In the end, we ruled out my crazy cousin Holbreth, who'd politically married into a wealthy family out in the north. There'd been rumors that he loved wealth more than anything else. The family he married into owned a massive silver mine, and he had no reason to leave.

My other cousin, Nathan, had become a marauder on the outskirts of the kingdom to keep roaming tribes off our lands while enjoying his fair share of looting and pillaging. He'd never attacked the kingdom. Edward immediately excluded him from the list, as he was simply too far away.

That left two possibilities, both of whom made me uneasy. Doyle and Etain each had a solid grasp of politics and what was needed to rule. Doyle was an offspring of my mother's mother and a drow. He embraced his drow heritage and focused mostly on their politics. Etain was interested in ruling through religious means and had made a name for herself by converting lands to the goddess for my father. Lately she'd been prevented from pursuing other lands so quickly and had shown her distaste at being repri-manded by my parents.

"Tell me more about this Doyle you keep coming back to. What is a drow? What type of politics are they involved with?" he asked. He closed his eyes while he listened to what I knew of them and their power structure.

"Drow are night elves with dark skin and light hair. They have two political strides: subterfuge and slavery. When they are fully committed, they go for the jugular in order to claim their prize." I leaned closer, enjoying his strong, masculine scent.

A smile played on his lips. "Yes, I know the type. Arro-gant, power-hungry, and disciplined. The dangerous sort." He lifted his stubbled chin, and his piercing eyes stared straight into mine.

There was a knock on the door, and Sir Alan walked in without waiting for approval. He leveled a suspicious glare at Edward. As if he'd do anything. Edward was more of a gentleman than many of the noblemen I'd seen at court. "Your Highness, Edward, I wanted to ensure everything was well here. Would you like some supper, Princess? I could have some sent up."

My mind had been so fixed on my family's politics that I'd forgotten about food. Sir Alan always looked after me, but I couldn't help to wonder if he had an ulterior motive for coming here. Was he jealous of Edward, or just wary of him? I wasn't sure, and to be honest, I couldn't allow myself to get distracted now. I felt that something kept eluding me during our conversation.

"I think the princess could use some dinner, Sir Alan," Edward said. "I'd appreciate you having it sent over. Your Highness, if you don't mind, I'll remain here and keep studying the political landscape a bit longer."

The thought of food made my stomach grumble. It had been a while since I'd eaten, and I could use a rest from talking. I knew we had to find the culprit, but having a break might clear my head. "I'll come downstairs with you, sir."

Edward gave a small nod before bowing back over the documents, as if there was more to glean from them than we'd already discussed.

On the way to the dining room and even while eating, Sir Alan was uncharacteristically quiet. Normally he spared a word of advice or encouragement, but today, he seemed tired and on edge. I leaned toward him a little and raised an eyebrow.

"Fine, Your Highness. I just don't know about you being in there all alone with him." He sighed. "While you two were in there, we caught two assassins sneaking up the tower on their way to the room you would've been staying in."

It seemed Edward's suggestion on which room to fortify

had been well founded. The assassins didn't know where I was. I was safe. He'd earned my trust twice now. Never mind that I found him irresistible, but even so... I turned my focus back onto Sir Alan again.

"Why didn't you tell me sooner?" I wasn't upset. Merely annoyed that he hadn't thought to tell me there'd been another attempt on my life. And this one had been inside a fortified location, where I was supposedly safe from the usual mercenaries everyone employed. That meant either they'd entered with a degree of influence and knowledge, or they bought off the guards.

A chill ran up my spine as it hit me. I knew who was behind this. "I'm sorry, but I have to go."

12

EDWARD

I looked around the study and tried to gather my thoughts. This room was filled with the knowledge of this world, and I only had to reach for a book to get a proper grasp of what was happening here politically. While we spoke a closely related language, actually reading their language gave me grief, but I muscled through as best as I could. I'd scribbled notes when Brigit told me of the political landscape and about her family. Beyond that, the volumes upon volumes of books would take forever for me to glean anything from.

Frustrated, I'd remained here to check the maps for landmarks. From what I'd heard, I knew where we were on the map, then it was easy to discover where our path would take us. A few smaller towns dotted the road with at least two big cities on the way over to the large castle that dominated the center of the map. Seats of power tended to be placed in the center. Even the Romans with all their world knowledge had the same hubris. Early British rulers hadn't been much better. Each feudal lord placed their seat of power at the center of their maps, and thus their own small worlds.

The door slammed open, and I spun around to see the princess rush in. Her eyes sparkled with excitement. Her sudden entry had taken me by surprise, and I'd already drawn my knife from my belt ready to strike.

She raised an eyebrow at me. "Don't be so jumpy. You might hurt someone." I wanted to shake her. There were assassins. I had to be watchful. As she neared, I noticed a slight blush on her cheeks. The curve of her form took my mind away from her words. "Edward, could you tell me what you wrote earlier?"

I read what we'd discussed about the possible trouble-makers. When I reached the end of Doyle's political focus being drow, she lifted her hand.

"The drow genuinely dislike half-breeds. My uncle can only rise so high in their society and can only achieve so much with them. He has the ambition and the skill, but he's held back by generations of traditions. With nowhere to grow in drow society, what if he's looking for another venue to establish his power?" Brigit pointed to the map.

"It's a bit of a leap to go from drow politics to murdering your parents." I rose from my seat to see where she was pointing. It slowly began to make sense. The distances and timing. "He had to wait." I cocked my head to the side and let my assassin's perspective kick in. "He's been waiting for this." A sense of dread slowly spread through my gut.

"What is it?" she asked, mirroring the tilt of my head as if it would help her see what I saw. Her hair swayed toward me, barely out of reach, and an urge to run my fingers through it nearly overtook my hands.

"He had to wait until you were far enough from the

throne to accomplish his plan. It means he's aware that we most likely sought shelter here. I overheard the guards saying that Sir Alan caught a few assassins climbing the stairs. We have to leave here soon." I strode back to the desk and began putting the books back in their places.

"What do you mean? We have to leave now? Please talk to me." The tone of her voice wasn't panicked. Instead, it carried dignity and mild confusion.

"He knows where we are. He can either send a small army against us and send reinforcements whenever needed, while buying more and more allegiance as we sit here help-lessly. Or he sets up multiple ambushes to stall us on our way to the throne, while mounting a proper assault, cutting off any chance to escape. We have a narrow window of opportunity if we leave right now. I'll reach out to Sir Alan. Be prepared." Tension tightened my shoulders, and I fought the need to brush my lips against hers before it might be too late. Instead, I opened the door and headed along the hallway to where Sir Alan was talking with his knights.

He was in a small room with Sir Orland and two other knights, each with a tankard of ale in their hands. "Sir Alan, we need to leave. Her life is in danger." The tone of my voice made it clear I wasn't joking.

"Did she send you here?" At my nod, he said, "Of course, Edward. I'll ready the troops."

"With all respect, sir, we should leave now with a small group that will escape attention. Five or six strong, and not a man more. The rest of the knights should remain here to stall our enemy's advancement."

His demeanor changed on the spot. "Absolutely not. I know you've wormed your way close to her, you knave, but this is going too far. It's my duty to keep her safe. I will not have her leave here with a handful of troops." He kept his voice low, but the animosity in it was obvious.

"You will be there to keep her safe, as will I. But men are needed here to make the enemy think we are still inside the keep." Diplomacy wasn't a strong suit of mine, but I restrained myself from yelling at him.

"The lad might be right. I give you my word that I'll keep the men safe and the enemy distracted." Sir Orlan slapped Sir Alan on the back. "Protect our princess. Despite what you may think of this man, he's been right so far. If he's half as smart as I think he is, then we'll all be in trouble for not listening sooner. Go on. Hopefully we'll see one another again."

"Thank you, sir. I wish you all the best." The knight was so casual in the way he'd given his word to keep the enemy busy, even if he had to sacrifice his life. It reminded me of tales I'd read of WWII veterans, knowing their chances were slim but still doing what they considered to be right.

"Keep this brave knight on the right path. He's slow to trust, but he would give his life for those he knows well. Farewell, Sir Alan." Without another word, Sir Orlan left the room. The other knights said their goodbyes as well and ventured after the older man.

I stood there for a moment with the fuming knight who'd just lost the sharp edge of his anger. Not eager to cause more conflict, I turned to leave.

"If this turns out to be a trick, Edward, know I'll have your hide. I'll gather a couple men. Meet me in the stables with the princess and her maidservant in a few moments." The knight shook his head and stormed down the hall.

I headed upstairs to gather my meager belongings before returning to Brigit. In the courtyard, I heard Sir

Orlan gathering his men to prepare for a siege. There were orders to block the outer gates and gather supplies to the keep's basement. Refocusing on my task, I jogged back to the study for Brigit. She was reading some dusty-looking tome as I entered, her focus solely on the text. "Come on, let's get out of here," I said and hefted her possessions.

It took a few minutes to gather Tabitha, some supplies, rations, and a smaller tent should we need it. Sir Orlan had passed Sir Alan a few gold coins in case we needed to strike bargains with the people on our way. Each of us had a cloak to hide ourselves in, and a different horse than we'd ridden in on. We took an escape tunnel underneath Skyhaven to the outside. There were six of us: Brigit, Tabitha, Sir Alan, two knights I didn't recognize, and me.

We were just travelers on our way to the capital now. To make things more believable, we split the supplies evenly between us. Sir Alan, to my surprise, also had a small lute that he occasionally played as if to make time pass quicker on the road.

To my culturally untrained eye, we seemed to blend in.

The small roads we were on slowly became wider and better maintained as we approached the main trade routes between the cities. Even as the roads merged, I began seeing suspicious activity that indicated possible ambushes were already being prepared.

Between the trees that lined the roads, I saw platforms that could be used for a lookout or an archer. Rope and sharpened sticks hung from trees, as if ready to ensnare an unwitting bystander.

Still, we kept riding along, not giving any indication of fear. Eventually the moon shone above us, and a nearby small town seemed be a wise stopping point. We didn't want to face bandits, and I doubted anyone in the small town would've seen the princess's face before. I only hoped Doyle and his agents were still unaware that we'd broken away from our main force. As we neared the town, the sights and smells of the place mixed with the lilting sound of singing. It didn't take long for us to find the local tavern.

13

BRIGIT

The tavern had several townsfolk in it, but thankfully, there were still rooms available. The town didn't seem to get many travelers. It might get some passing through as we were, but it wasn't a center of activity. Not that it mattered to me. I was just grateful that we were off the road. Horseback riding was enjoyable enough when done on occasion, but it was becoming ever more tiring. It took all my strength to remain in the saddle during the last few hours of our ride.

Part of me wanted to go directly to my room, clean up, and fall asleep, but all the horseback riding had stirred my hunger. The tavern might not serve food on par with my family's castle, but it would be better than what I was used to getting on the road...hopefully.

Our group sat in a corner with Edward and Sir Alan keeping an eye on the door. Tabitha remained quiet for once. Perhaps she was tired from our travels too. The other knights talked amongst themselves, but I tuned their conversation out. The cloak's hood covered the top of my face, and I reached for the brim to push it back.

Edward caught my wrist and shook his head slightly. His warm hand on me sent shivers up my arm. "Not yet," he said in a low voice so no one at the other tables could hear.

"Right. I'm sorry." I took a sip of ale, doing my best to cope with the hood. It was a challenge, but I managed. No one could know who I was here. If they found out, word would reach Doyle.

We weren't sure who was feeding him information about me, but the fact he'd known where I was every step of the way so far disturbed me. Who had betrayed us? Were they among me now? I looked at Tabitha, Edward, Sir Alan, and the two other knights with me. While I didn't know who they were, I trusted Sir Alan's judgment in bringing them along. He had never let me down before, even if he wasn't happy that Edward was helping us. He didn't seem to trust Edward much, but I did.

I looked between the two of them. Their faces were stoic as they sat there like two sentinels. I shook my head and focused on the delicious ale, finishing off a tankard in barely no time at all before waving for the bar wench to bring me another. The second one went down just as easily as the first, and by that time, our food had arrived and with it another ale.

The food tasted great. I'd never eaten so quickly in all my life. Perhaps I'd been hungrier than I realized. The ale had quenched my palate, and I choked on a giggle. The alcohol made me a little lightheaded and giddy. I typically didn't drink so heavily when I was in the castle, but this seemed as good a time as any to imbibe. It wasn't as if I had anything else to do but cower in fear from Doyle.

I clenched my hands into fists at the thought of his name and pushed back from the table, nearly tipping over as I did. My knees trembled, but Tabitha steadied me. I shoved her hands away. We were just a group of travelers. I couldn't be having someone dote on me. That would draw attention to us, and we both knew it.

Tabitha's lips curved into a frown from beneath her hood, but she didn't say anything. She remained quiet and seated, letting me retire to my room alone. We were sharing a room. It was better to stick together, especially since Edward and Sir Alan likely wanted someone to keep an eye on me at all times. I grimaced as I turned my back on them.

It took all of my focus to place one foot in front of the other and not teeter over. The hallway to the rooms blurred a little, and I tried to remember which one was supposed to be mine. There was one for Sir Alan, one for the two knights, one for Edward, and one for Tabitha and me. I leaned against the wall and stared at the four doors, willing them to let me in on their secrets.

When they didn't, I picked the door closest to me. All of the rooms were decorated in a similar fashion. I couldn't be sure if I'd picked the right one. However, my body was weak and drunk. I didn't really care if this was my designated room or not. I pulled off the heavy cloak and tossed it to the floor, along with as much of the armor they'd saddled me with as I could, before collapsing onto the bed. The moment my head hit the pillow, I was fast asleep. Not even dreams intruded on my drunken stupor.

"Princess?" A voice stirred me from sleep.

"Go away." I turned to face the wall, not wanting to be disturbed.

"You're in my room. I can't." The crisp, masculine tone held a hint of humor.

I jerked into a sitting position, instantly regretting the sudden movement as nausea swept over me.

Edward sat beside me on the bed. His gaze remained

trained on my face, but as I moved, he let it slide lower. Heat filled his eyes, and he jerked his attention back to my face. "I'm sorry to disturb you..."

I glanced down to see what he saw. My pants were gone. The only clothing on me was the leather armor covering my chest and my undergarments. "Um, I think I'm the one who should be sorry." I tried to pull the blanket over me, but we were sitting on it. Besides, I wasn't exactly unhappy to be here with him. I'd never been in a state of undress with a man before, but Edward didn't make me feel improper or vulnerable.

"No need to apologize. It's fine. Here, let's get you to your room." He rose to his feet and helped me up. My legs gave out from the still potent buzz I had, and I careened into his chest, clinging to his armor. He wrapped his arms around my waist, and warmth curled into the pit of my stomach. He held me close, even when I'd regained my footing.

I glanced up at him and ran my fingertips over the stubble covering his strong jawline. He was more handsome than any man I'd ever seen before. Before I knew what I was doing, I rose on tiptoes and pressed a kiss against his lips.

Edward stiffened beneath my touch, and fear raked its claws over me. Had I been too bold? I hardly ever let go of my inhibitions. Now I had firsthand experience of why I shouldn't.

I pulled back a little. "My apologies. I—"

But he didn't release me. Instead, he covered my mouth with his. His lips brushed against mine, and the tip of his tongue slid over my lower lip as if beckoning me to open my mouth for him. When I did, he moved in slowly, as if we had all the time in the world. He ran his hands up my back and stripped away the leather armor, only pulling away enough to push it down my shoulders.

"I've wanted you ever since..." He stopped and shook his head. "For a while now. If you don't feel the same, I won't pressure you into this."

I didn't respond. I didn't need to. I just wrapped my arms around his shoulders and savored his warm embrace as I trailed my tongue over his lower lip. Desire for him tightened my core, and I wanted to be with him more than I'd wanted anything in a long time. Perhaps our paths were meant to cross. The doors between realms were precise and always did what they chose to do for a reason.

Edward wrapped his arms around my waist, and he leaned in to place kisses against my neck and shoulders. I couldn't suppress a moan as he nipped the tender flesh of my throat. My body burned with him this close. I wanted things I'd never really known I could have before.

I slid my hands over his broad chest, feeling his tight muscles coil beneath my touch. What would it be like to feel his hot skin against mine? I leaned up on my tiptoes to kiss him again.

My people didn't favor consummating relationships before the wedding night, but part of me wasn't sure if I'd ever have a chance to partake in those festivities. My own uncle...

I shook that thought from my mind. Now wasn't the time to think of all we'd learned. I would deal with him once I reached my family's castle. For now, I could only take solace in Edward's arms. He'd protected me time and again, and I cared for him in a way I'd never felt before.

He slid his hands down my waist to my backside, and his hot palms kneaded the muscles there, soothing me as he walked me back toward the bed. "You're sure about this, princess?" he asked, pulling away a little.

"Yes."

Edward pulled me closer. "Close your eyes and indulge in the sensations, love. Be with me in this moment."

"I'm sorry. I... It's hard knowing my own family is plotting against me. That my uncle might have killed my parents." I bit my lower lip. "I want this. I want what we have together. Please."

He stared into my eyes. "Take a few deep breaths with me and clear your mind." He drew in a deep breath before letting it out, then drew in another in a calming, rhythmic pattern. I followed his lead, and just as he'd said, the deep breaths seemed to relax my body and mind. "That really does work." I smiled at him in wonder.

"Yes, it does."

I could kick myself for ruining the moment. Who knew if this would be one of our last moments of safety and reprieve before pressing onto my family's castle? We were alone, and in between Tabitha and Sir Alan, that was hard to manage.

I untied the cord on his leather armor, wanting to see his skin and press my bare chest against it. He watched my fingers move, and the slow burn of heat in his eyes glowed like embers. I wanted to fan myself just being this near to him.

He dropped his armor onto the floor beside us and started stripping away his other clothes, putting his knife and gun in a safe spot near the head of the bed.

I wrapped my arms around his waist when he was done and pressed kisses against his massive chest. He moaned, and the sound rumbled against my lips, making me giggle. He ran his fingertips through my hair and caressed the back of my head.

I trailed my hands lower, feeling his abdomen clench beneath my touch, then untied his leather pants. Glancing up at him, I hesitated for a moment, unsure what to do since I'd never been intimate with a man. I'd read stories and heard from those at the court that women were basically there to make heirs. They lay on their backs and let the man have their way with them to reproduce. That didn't ring true with the desire that welled within me and moistened my thighs. There was more between Edward and me than merely procreating.

"No need to be bashful, princess." Edward's warm voice made me smile, and he placed his hands gently over mine as we pushed the leather pants away. "We'll not get far by keeping them on, and I intend to do more than just kiss and pet you." He pulled me toward the bed, and I glanced down to see his thick shaft protruding from his body.

My eyes widened a little, and I ran my fingertips over him enjoying his groans of pleasure.

"That's dangerous." He placed his hand over mine and leaned me back on the bed. "I want to explore your body and take my time getting to know you intimately." His thumbs hooked into my undergarments as he flashed me a handsome grin.

Our bodies came together in a whirlwind of pleasure. We indulged ourselves in one another's bodies. I muffled my cries in Edward's passionate kisses for fear the knights would barge in, but no one bothered us. This night was one of the best I'd ever experienced. Edward had opened up new worlds to me. I only hoped we lived through the coming weeks, so we could make many more of these sacred moments.

14

EDWARD

The past few days had left me exhausted, both physically and mentally. I hadn't planned on developing feelings for a woman I hadn't known for long, but I couldn't help but feel warmth burn in my chest when I thought of her.

While I wouldn't mind remaining here and exploring our newfound emotions for each other, we had to press on. I wasn't sure if the group knew what transpired between us, but I wanted to keep what we had private, just in case.

Tabitha sat down next to me, and the look she gave us signaled that she knew something. It made sense, really, because Brigit had only returned to her room early this morning. But what did it matter if she did? I hadn't done anything with the princess that she hadn't wanted me to.

I turned my attention back to my breakfast and thought of how I'd gotten into this mess. I'd gone through a door without much choice, protected a princess, got caught in a power grab, and now had isolated her from her troops, leaving us in the middle of nowhere between Skyhaven and the kingdom's capital.

"We have some news about your uncle," Sir Alan said, keeping the reverence in his voice, even if he had to omit the words linking Brigit to her proper position. "It seems he's moving around the kingdom toward Darkview with his eyes on...some poor man's house. I swear, unless he keeps his head down, he'll make some powerful enemies there," he said, trying to mask his message. None of that was news. It was just as I'd expected, but I hated being right.

"My uncle has a way with people, though. He's not afraid to use his charms to sway opinions." Brigit frowned as she tore off another piece of bread.

I thought extortion, torture, blackmail, and outright murder were more likely. He seemed like an experienced player of dirty politics, who would use any means to achieve his ends.

I stole a glance between the two of them. Their attempt at being discreet was nice, but it'd fool no one if the right person overheard them. "You might as well plant a sign out there. Neither of you are being subtle. I'm sure the trade routes have more than enough merchants for us to trade with instead. There's no need to venture all the way out to him to state our business. Why not sell the mining claim to one of the fancy nobles riding their groomed, tall horses?" Both of them stared at me as if I'd lost my mind.

I glared at them, hoping they'd take the hint.

Tabitha nudged my foot. At least she knew how to play the game.

But we all needed to be more aware of our words. Even slipping the word uncle into the conversation would be plain enough for anyone who knew her family history. Even though the tavern was mostly empty, we didn't know how extensive Doyle's network of helpers was. After all, he'd had years to prepare for this.

"That's not all I've heard," one of the knights who'd taken the night shift piped up. "There were travelers here late last night. There are rumors of some old prince moving to claim the throne. They say his claim is true, and that we've never been led by a queen alone." He rubbed at his bleary eyes before sipping on his tankard of ale. "Not that it really matters, but it seems the current heir is indisposed. Freehaven needs someone to sit on the throne. Those who are against his claim have supposedly found themselves in a dungeon or taken away into foreign lands. I'd watch my tongue out there."

"When did you hear this?" Sir Alan asked him with a sharpness to his tone. Apparently, that hadn't been shared among the rest of the group yet. However, I was happy he chose not to intrude late last night with this news. It would've been quite compromising.

"What's done is done. Our investment should be safe, regardless of who sits on the throne. I'm sure in the end it'll all work out. What are our plans for today? Head out on the trade route to find yet another tavern by the evening?" I asked, keeping my gaze on Sir Alan's.

He glanced around the table before nodding. "Yes. We should get on the road as soon as possible." He pushed his empty plate away from him. "Daylight is wasting, and we have quite a distance to go." As the knights went to pay the bartender, I took a moment to lean closer to Tabitha. She'd been quiet this morning.

"I hope I haven't offended you." I meant it. Brigit and her maid had a kind of friendship between them, and I didn't want to be the cause of friction.

"You spent the evening with her. I'm not as blind or as deaf as the knights. The two of you should keep quiet next time. The amount of giggling that came through the walls woke me a few times." I felt the slight press of her blade against my thigh. "The one thing I really care about is that you don't harm her. If you do, no amount of training will save you from me. She's more important to me than everyone in the keep we left behind, and you've dragged her into danger's path. While our knights kept an eye on the tavern and drank, I watched what was going on outside." Tabitha fixed her gaze on Brigit across the table. "A few messengers entered and left the town. That's not normal. Yesterday on the road there were very few travelers or messengers. A few of them spoke amongst themselves near the stables across the road. With the tavern's noise, I couldn't make out much, but something happened at Skyhaven. Something bad."

Brigit's eyes widened, and her mouth opened but no words came out.

Within the half hour, we'd taken our belongings and paid the staff for their hospitality. The town's blacksmith had repaired the shoes on one of the horses, and Sir Alan had a relaxed chat with the man. It wasn't hard to imagine him as a blacksmith's apprentice in his youth with his wide, strong frame.

When we finally hit the road, he shared what he'd learned. Apparently the messengers had run their horses so hard their shoes had needed repair, too. The blacksmith had been awoken in the middle of the night to help the men. They bragged amongst themselves about working with someone from the royal family who'd paid well for their services. After everything was said and done, the messengers departed in a hurry, but not before letting slip that they were searching for a group of men with a young woman among them. They were slowly closing in on us.

I scouted ahead first, riding a quarter mile ahead of the

others to ensure we weren't blindsided by Doyle's minions. For the first half of the day, nothing happened, then I began to see incoming troops. The banners in the distance were my first warning. They had Doyle's colors on them with an angry red-eyed scorpion staring into cloudy skies.

Hidden behind a bend in the road, I turned the horse and galloped away. We barely had enough time to move everyone, including the horses, out of sight from the road to a nearby dry riverbed. As the troops marched by, I became aware of just how many mercenaries Doyle had been able to recruit. There were easily a thousand infantry, not counting his mounted force.

My mind returned to the brave men at Skyhaven. I only hoped Sir Orlan would be able to maintain his hold on the keep a while longer. It was now only a matter of time before it would fall. Even as we moved the horses back up the muddy embankment, I had a hard time keeping my thoughts clear. Fifty of the princess's men, plus whoever had been stationed in the keep, against a thousand. If Sir Orlan was a wise man, he'd surrender to keep his troops alive, but he'd given his word to buy us as much time as he could.

Sir Alan eagerly took the next turn to scout for us, perhaps to have time alone to think. The group continued on our way solemnly along the dusty road. The clouds above darkened, and it wasn't long until thunder could be heard in the distance. It would likely rain soon. If we didn't find shelter, we'd be caught in the open on the road. Sir Alan returned after a few moments with the storm front nearly on top of us.

"We need to get off the road," Sir Alan yelled to be heard over the sound of thunder.

We had no clear insight to which direction we should go.

The nearest cover was a forest not far off, but it wouldn't be enough.

The two knights broke off from the group in a search of shelter, while I remained with the women and Sir Alan. A few wet minutes passed before they returned with good news. There was a small cave not far away, dry and out of sight. Hail started pelting us as we rode hard to its much-needed protection.

With their guidance, we tied our horses beneath a thick set of trees and ducked inside. There were no signs of local wildlife in the tiny cave, and within a few moments, Sir Alan had started a small fire. We all sat around it as we shared rations and tried to warm up.

Strangely enough, I was relatively happy. I was near someone I'd do anything to protect.

15

EDWARD

The rest of the evening had been lost to heavy rain. Lightning and hail made it impossible to travel more than a few feet from the cave's entrance to retrieve more wood. The knights had taken turns doing that and set the wet wood close to the fire so it could be used later. Tabitha and Sir Alan had the foresight to use their cloaks to block the fire's light from leaving the cave. It was unlikely Doyle's little spies were roaming the countryside, but not impossible, if they were paid enough. During a night like this, a fire would draw immediate attention. A brief respite came as we boiled water and brewed a light tea by using pine needles and berries that had been close to the cave.

Along with the tea, rations of cheese and bread kept everyone happy and alert. I took the first hour's watch, which mostly consisted of listening to the flames and ensuring they didn't go out. Before I knew it, Sir Alan relieved me, and I fell asleep against the wall with one hand on my sword's hilt.

Morning light and the smell of porridge woke me up. I'd

been dreaming of bacon, eggs, and scones, but to my stomach, it made no difference. Even with everyone being so crammed together, I found a couple of chances to gently touch Brigit's elbow or hips as we maneuvered around for food, and then when we packed everything up to leave again. She gave me a knowing smile.

Outside, the weather had cleared, and the storm's power was plainly evident in the state of the forest. Broken branches, beaten bushes, and bark-stripped trees lined our path back to the road.

There was mud everywhere, and although the blazing sun was out in the valley. It glinted against pools of murky water on the ground. Puddles, holes, and other such environmental problems would be abundant, making it hard to know what to trust. We couldn't let a horse break its leg at this point in our journey. Although it was painstakingly slow to guide them, it'd end up saving us time in the end.

Sir Alan was first to scout ahead. It wasn't long until he returned with news that a small company of men were fast approaching. As he neared us, his face went suddenly pale.

I didn't have to turn because I could hear the heavy trampling of horses from somewhere behind us. We were flanked. *Shite*. There were no bushes, or trees, or anything useful around. In the distance were small hills, but in our immediate vicinity, we had no protection and were on a patch of road that could prove hazardous for our horses.

"What should we do?" Tabitha asked, the slightest tinge of fear evident in her voice.

"What we can. We need to split up and hope they go after the wrong people, or that enough of us manage to escape." I knew the chances of getting away were slim to none, but we didn't have any other option. I turned my horse toward the grasslands and saw Sir Alan hesitantly steer his in the opposite direction.

"Keep her safe," Sir Alan shouted before taking off, making a wide arch to get around the riders behind us.

Without any more hesitation, we began to split up. I rode past a few boulders and heard another horse make its way toward me. Taking a look over my shoulder, I saw Tabitha and Brigit following me. In the distance, Sir Alan had managed to draw a sizable portion of the cavalry his way. The other two knights had branched off to the opposite side of the road, pushing their horses into a similar arc. It wasn't enough. Some of the cavalry officers remained on our tails.

"Fuck it." I let out an exasperated grunt. It was useless to deny what would eventually happen anyway. "Brigit, Tabitha, keep going straight for those hills," I yelled over my shoulder and began to pull my horse to the side. My gun might not have many bullets, but maybe it'd act as a deterrent. Dismounting, I took aim at the first horse and pulled the trigger. The huge beast went down, causing a small pileup as the horses behind it stumbled into it. Knowing I wouldn't have a lot of time, I fired two more bullets into the fray, hoping it'd drive some common sense into the heavily armored men.

I mounted my horse again and pushed the stallion into a gallop. The horse lurched as one of its legs went into a pothole that had looked like just another puddle. A horrible snap sounded as it fell. I had a moment of weightlessness before a sharp pain stabbed the side of my head. Everything went dark for a few moments.

When I awoke, I kept my eyes closed and my body unmoving. I took extremely shallow breaths at a controlled pace, grateful for the cloak that covered most of my chest and masked its movement.

"He seems dead, sir. Let's leave this one and find the rest. This one might've gotten off lucky from what I've heard of our new king's plans for the group." A man spoke near my head, in a hard-to-understand accent.

"Yes. Leave the corpse. We don't need more dead weight. There isn't much time to set up a pyre. Gather the men. We still have the bitch to catch. Remember, he wants her unharmed. I don't care if she stabs you. You won't lift a finger against her."

"Damn it. I can't stand to watch that horse suffer. You there! End that one. I don't care the idiot ran him like that, but we should give the horse some peace."

The men grumbled as one of them dropped into a crouch next to the injured horse beside me. It took all my self-control not to flinch as the man cut the horse's throat and its blood sprayed hot over me. Whoever these mercenaries were, at least they cared for the horses and seemed loyal to whoever bought them. It was more than some people I'd dealt with in the past. They didn't seem to have an unreasonable bloodlust of injuring their enemy's corpses.

It didn't take long before the cavalry moved on. The vibration of their horses' hooves no longer carried through the ground, but I hesitated to move. If they didn't already have her, they likely would soon. I'd failed to protect her. Failed on a mission for the first time, ever.

With my horse dead, and quite a distance from Dark-view, I'd never make it in time. Tears dampened my cheeks. I'd let myself get close to her, and now she was gone. I had no way of reaching her. Despite all I'd done, it had been useless.

What are you going to do about it? Cry and hope it'll all work out? Get on your feet. The woman you love doesn't have much time left, and if you don't save her, no one will.

I opened my eyes. I was an assassin. Those who dared hurt her would die. I wasn't some sniveling peasant pushed aside and forgotten. I served my princess, and those who stood in my way had better move aside. The journey might be long, but so what? My feet might blister, my body might ache, but I was still alive. While I still drew breath, I would do everything in my power to save her.

Climbing to my feet took effort, but the more I moved, the more energy returned to me. I knew what direction I had to go, and with the training I'd had, this should be easy. I patted my pockets but couldn't find my gun. It took several minutes before I located it, and I breathed a sigh of relief. The horse still carried some supplies, mostly water and dry rations. I took what I could from the saddlebags. My cloak had been torn to the point of uselessness, but I took it along to help stave off the cold during the nights to come.

16

BRIGIT

I hated leaving Edward behind, but I knew I had to push on. He'd risked his life for mine. The future of the kingdom depended on me getting away. Tabitha, bless her, noticed when the cavalry took a turn toward us. Thankfully, they refrained from using their bows. It seemed that their instructions were to take us hostage. The idea of being caught by mercenaries wasn't pleasant, but it'd be better than outright dying.

Our initial lead on the mercenaries closed as our horses began to get tired. We'd pushed them harder than we should have, and the storm had taken its toll. Already beaten by hail and tired from the day's ride, the horses were little match for the trained cavalry's fresh horses.

"They'll catch us soon enough, Your Highness. When they do, you can't resist. They might kill us if you do. The less aggravated they are, the better for both of us." Tabitha pulled one of her knives from her satchel and hid it inside her clothing. It seemed she had no intention of being violated without having a chance to fight back.

They caught us within a few more minutes, cutting off our escape, and forcing us to dismount.

One of the officers wore the regalia of Doyle's cause. He appeared to be in charge. He had an air of arrogance to him, but was also attentive, a dangerous combination in an enemy's follower. It meant he was dedicated to thoroughly completing his mission no matter what.

"Come with me peacefully, princess. I don't wish to hurt you. I was instructed to bring you back with me alive. There was no indication what condition you should be in, so long as your face is unharmed and you're capable of providing an heir for my lord." His words shook me to the core. This was far worse than anything I'd imagined. Not only would I be dragged away to Doyle, but I was supposed to surrender my kingdom to him and provide him an heir.

My legs trembled, but I forced myself to stay upright. "I'll come with you. Please, just don't hurt my maidservant." I reached for Tabitha, but the officer before me grabbed my hand and pulled me away from her.

"So long as you don't give me any reasons to look unfavorably upon her, I'll try to make sure she's unharmed. You're the only one my lord cares about." He winked at Tabitha, then lifted me onto his horse. "Gerald, take this one with you." He pointed at Tabitha. "Try not to have too much fun."

The other mercenary stalked forward and grabbed Tabitha by the upper arm, yanking her in the direction of his horse without a word. Tears formed in Tabitha's eyes, and my shoulders slumped forward. All of this was my fault. Perhaps if I'd taken a larger force to storm my family's castle, none of this would be happening now. Instead, I'd tried to use stealth, and my uncle had continued to outwit me. What good was I as the Queen of Freehaven if I couldn't even evade capture?

My heart lurched in my chest as I thought of Edward, Sir Alan, and the other two knights. Had they even managed to make it out alive? What if they were dead? All because they were trying to protect me. Was my life worth them giving theirs away?

The officer climbed onto the horse behind me, but I barely paid him any attention. My turbulent thoughts kept me occupied as we rode toward Darkview.

How could I have been so stupid?

Tears threatened to spill from my eyes, but I held them in check. I suddenly wished for the obnoxiously oversized cloak to hide my face again. At least I would've been able to sort through my emotions in private. The men who'd captured me and Tabitha pushed their horses hard as they rode. What seemed to have taken a lot longer on the journey to my cousin's stronghold was over by nightfall. We'd ridden almost the whole day, but it meant I'd have this chapter in my life closed sooner than later.

Perhaps I could bargain with Doyle. I could meet with my advisors and give him something he wanted. A title or some land? What was it he'd wanted from my mother and father that caused the rift in our family? I shook the thought away, unable to remember. My mother hadn't spoken of that time in her life much.

We rode through the front gates, and I saw violence all around me. The men and women who lived in the capital were being abused by Doyle's mercenaries. This wasn't the way to treat people, but perhaps he didn't care. He was a slaver, after all. Would my people become his slaves too?

Nausea overwhelmed me, and I clenched my stomach, feeling a prick of pain as my fingers brushed the spot on my side where I'd been narrowly cut. I bit my lower lip to hold in a cry.

The people around us stopped what they were doing and started shouting. "Princess! Princess! Help us, Princess!"

I lowered my head, not wanting to look at them. How could I help them when I couldn't even help myself? "I'm sorry," I muttered under my breath.

The officer behind me leaned in a little. "Don't be so glum. Act like a princess for them, not a coward. They look up to you. You're only making yourself appear weaker."

I turned a little in the saddle to look at him, but regardless of his loyalty to my uncle, he was right. If I acted like a prisoner, my people might lose all hope. That was the last thing they needed right now. "I'm beaten and your prisoner, what do you care?" I spit the words at him with venom in my tone.

"It's not for you, but for them. They need to have faith that there is still hope for the future. Furthermore, you've been captured. You're not dead yet, Princess. Trust me. There are things worse than death, but as long as you live, you are bound to the kingdom. How dare you let your people down? Some here still remember your father and the sacrifices your family made to ensure Freehaven's safety. Some of us don't have the option to stand up and fight against our lord, but that doesn't mean we're bad people." He grinned. "You'd be amazed to know how many follow him due to blackmail and his iron fist. None have stood up and said 'enough' yet. When that happens, his line of pledged officers will likely abandon him." The officer spoke in whispers, but his demeanor was outwardly arrogant as if he was nothing more than a commander in Doyle's army.

Passion resonated in his words, and some of them matched what my father had taught me. Humility, honesty, and duty to your kingdom were the cornerstones of my family. The officer was right. I'd let the people down if I rolled over for Doyle. Despite the situation, I was still the princess of Freehaven, and the kingdom's rightful ruler.

I was beaten but alive, and my people needed me more than ever. I pushed down the pain and my fear of what was to come and put on a brave face as I looked into the crowd.

There was a subtle change in the masses as I did. None of the guards near me seemed to notice, but the beaten-down people began to pull themselves together slowly. A crying mother holding her child walked away with determination on her face. A desperate blacksmith with his hammer clutched in his left hand lifted it with renewed hope.

"The seeds of rebellion are born out of bravery and tyranny," the officer said as he reinforced the idea in my head.

Doyle was a slaver, a tyrant. As long as I was alive, the people had reason for hope. And as long as they had hope, they'd push back against his new rule. He might sit on the throne, but he would not rule the kingdom. The people might pay his taxes, but they'd hide their profits. The sons and daughters that he'd draft and train would rise against him with cold resentment in their hearts.

It was a bittersweet realization.

I wasn't worthy to have such people looking up to me. I was one woman. They'd sacrifice their lives for a cause but would likely have little impact. Their deaths would be meaningless as long as I was his captive. Doyle knew this, too. The moment he had an heir, he wouldn't need me alive anymore. He'd execute me. Without a worthy cause, the people would slowly surrender and let go of their hope. Either way, innocent lives would be lost for an ideal, an icon.

I didn't want to become their martyr. But if the people had nothing to believe in, they'd lose hope. If they lost hope, the kingdom would lose its soul, and its future would fall into the hands of a tyrant.

The officer turned my head and raised his eyebrow at me. "It seems you've begun to understand what it means to rule. There are many tyrants, but few rulers." He released my face and stared back into the crowd. For a moment I thought I recognized him. A scar ran along his chin that reminded me of a knight who'd been banished from my father's court when I was young. His name eluded me, but I knew I'd have lots of time to think about it.

We rode on in silence to the grand castle looming over us. The great walls that had once kept me safe would now be my prison. On the pristine grey stone hung the bodies of loyal knights, displayed to show everyone the price of loyalty for the old king.

Guards stood along the road with sunken eyes as they continued on their duties without looking up at the oncoming riders. It wasn't until we'd reached the courtyard that a soft murmur seemed to grow.

"It's her." The whispers spread from those handling the horses onward, like a wave racing toward a beach.

Doyle strode out into the courtyard with a grin on his pitch-black face. His bodyguard of drow mercenaries wore skull-shaped helmets. Their piercing red eyes shone like fire and were enough to intimidate anyone who dared get too close. Each of them carried a greatsword and had an assortment of smaller blades attached to their belts, as if prepared for any kind of combat.

Doyle wore a deep green tinted mail. His features might have been handsome if they weren't twisted. His lips seemed to curve in a permanent grimace. His face likely reflected his corrupted soul, but saying something like that wouldn't be wise. Both of us knew he needed me alive for the time being, but I wasn't going to make it easy for him.

"Welcome home, my princess. You've had a long ride. Please, follow me to your chambers. There won't be a trial today, since I know you need your rest. Come over here, girl. There's no need to be shy with your uncle. I'm just doing what the kingdom needs." His voice carried easily around the courtyard, but his tone held no warmth. It was like the blast of a cold wind.

I was under no illusions about what he thought the kingdom needed. But what he wanted wasn't right. Dread built within me, but I forced my face into a disinterested expression as a way to defy him.

"What do you mean by trials, dearest uncle? I'm sure you and your pathetic claim to the throne should be the one in front of our judges," I said, keeping my voice calm. It would do little, but even the tiniest of barbs could fester.

"That's strange. I'm merely here to ensure Freehaven's safety. After all, you must've been driven mad with grief for being so far from your precious parents when they died. That's why you abandoned your duty to the kingdom and roamed the countryside. You're a traitor, and you'll be beheaded for shirking your duties. The trial might take years, though. As such, I'll merely act as Regent, for now." This time his voice carried a hint of humor.

The outside temperature seemed to drop as a shiver chased down my spine. The meaning of his words punched me in the gut. He didn't plan to claim the throne for himself. He would get me pregnant and have his heir take it instead.

17

EDWARD

I'd walked all day and all night on the road, going as far as it went until I found myself at a large city. Each gate had a number of guards to check the people and trade goods that entered. They most likely worked for Doyle. While I had no regalia belonging to Brigit, there was still a chance that one of the knights or the women had been tortured and my description was common knowledge. Still, it was a risk I'd have to take.

I pulled the tattered cloak tighter around me and waited in the small line to enter the city. The merchants in front of me were discussing the sudden demand for nuts and food for horses, as well as rumors about increased drafting in the outlying cities. They were also complaining about the return of an outdated vassalage system that would bind the hands of the nobles and give more power to the king. So, Doyle was recruiting more troops and making it harder for the nobles to turn against him. A noble without a substantial army would be noble in name alone.

The discussion had taken so much of my attention that I didn't notice one of the guards approach me from the side. I halted my movement and took half a step back to let the guard cross the road. I kept my head low, but my eyes alert. The guard went by without stopping, and I breathed a small sigh of relief.

A few minutes later, I was talking to the city guards themselves. They asked my business in the city, and I explained I was merely on a pilgrimage between the cities of the Founders. It was something I'd seen in Brigit's books, but if they pressed me on the subject, I'd be at a loss on what to say. I had no idea who or what the Founders were or even which cities they had founded. It was a big gamble.

The guards shook their heads before waving me through with no apparent interest. As I walked by, one of the guards called after me, "The city is under curfew, pilgrim. Don't remain outside after dusk."

Damn. Although, the rooftops and filthy underground of any city might remain active despite the law. *Or to spite it.*

I waved to the guard in thanks and walked along the road. It seemed my tattered clothes and bruised body had some use after all. I spent time familiarizing myself with the layout of the city. From the map I'd seen while at Skyhaven, I remembered the general quarters and sections of the city. Market squares were plentiful, but the biggest one was almost a third of the way into the city itself.

The castle dominated the landscape. Its moat and the natural protection of its elevated location made it an imposing structure. Even from this distance, I could see that catapults were slowly being built on the walls as if to warn everyone nearby that attacking the castle would be futile. The outer wall of the city formed a secondary wall around the castle's own, creating a double-ringed structure capable of withstanding significant damage, but they were also on levels so that if the city walls were lost, the invaders would be unable to use them to strongly attack the castle itself.

With no clue of where to go, I headed to the nearest tavern and asked where the thieves and burglars met. I used my pilgrimage story again, trying to convey that I was asked to deliver blessings to the poor and the outlaws that lived inside the city. After all, even they needed help, right?

As I lacked any significant amount of coin, I took my chances and liberated some from a few more inebriated men in the tavern. I'd built up a healthy buzz before the barkeep finally relented and gave me directions, for the price of four copper pieces. Knowing full well the bartender had seen the coins I carried, I was prepared for an ambush.

The bartender hesitated in the alley, which was my cue.

I whirled around, pressing a dagger to his soft stomach before the man had time to figure out what happened. Three shadows in the alley hardened before they walked closer to the mouth of the alley.

"Listen here, friend. There are more of us than you." A voice came from the figures in the darkness, carrying no annoyance, merely giving a cold statement of facts and a promise of what would unfold if I pushed harder.

I simply sent the bartender away and sheathed my knife beneath my cloak. "Good. I thought you might be amateurs. Do you want to see a queen on the throne, or are we going to argue about business proposals until the guards hear us?" My voice carried enough force to make the nearest merchants skitter away.

Quick footsteps sounded a moment before I was dragged into the shadows.

My guides' eyesight was good. I had a hard time catching all the turns and twists we made, but my nose was surprisingly good at helping me with the directions.

Beneath the smells of rot and decay in the alley, I noticed the spices and yeast, which was quickly followed by the smell of manure. By the time we'd made our fourth turn in the alleys, I smelled old mortar and that distinguished smell made from cooling metal in oil. We'd passed the markets and the bakeries, moved behind the working class and the stables and ended up somewhere close to the smithy, but there was an earthy and rough smell of oak in the air. While I'd have no way of really knowing my way around at least I was somewhat privy to my general location.

Eventually I was sat down in a rough wooden chair and a candle was lit. The workshop slowly took shape around me as my sight adjusted to the painfully bright candle that obscured more than it showed. Whoever was behind this knew how eyes worked, and they had common sense to remain outside of the circle of illumination that tried to keep the darkness at bay.

"So, was it really needed to push me to the carpenter's area?" I asked, keeping my tone neutral. From the cough coming from the other side, I knew I was mostly accurate in my estimation.

"Less ears and eyes out here." The speaker's accent carried a slight Slavic tone to it with the accentuated 's' that he used. I wasn't sure if he had a lisp or if this was just some local accent. Never the less, it made it slightly harder to fully follow his speech.

"Makes sense," I continued and rolled my shoulders that were roughly handed during my transit. "And, more to the point, moving me around would ensure that if I had worked for someone local, anyone following me would have to move past your guards. When they'd finally get here, they'd just find me sitting here, my throat cut as a warning, am I right?" I asked, remembering how Asian mob tended to prefer to do their business.

"Naturally. Now, let's discuss business. You stated that there'd be a way to avoid a small calamity in our future. Surely you know what that drow pretender would do if he gets his wish. We harbor no illusions what kind of treatment he'd give to us," another voice, this time behind me came surprisingly loud.

"Of course, I want to keep Her Majesty safe and sound. You want to get rid of Doyle. Those two goals are aligned. I already dealt with a few threats to Her Majesty's life, but alas, I was not able to stop him from taking her. And I presume that all of you would prefer that she will remain unaware of this little gathering group. That puts you all in an interesting place. While you want to secure your own interests, showing yourself openly would just draw more ire from the nobility in the long run." The words came easy. Action, that would be the harder part.

Murmur grew behind the candle, as more sources of light were lit and spread around the room. I saw a few beggars leaning against the beams that supported the workshop roof. To my right were what I presumed the thieves, clad in darkened, but regular clothing that would allow them to blended in the crowds with ease. And to my left were a mismatch collection of thugs. Each group had seemingly a speaker that sat on the other side of the original candle. Two of them had crossbows aimed at me, and the third had an interestingly long throwing knife at his side.

"I presume you got the word I wasn't followed?" I finally asked them and relaxed in the chair more. Without a word the crossbows were turned aside, and a few loaves of bread were brought in. The loaves were broken around the room, and I was offered a piece as well.

"We hear your suggestion. Now, let us fill in some details for you. This will not be easy." The beggar's leader coughed a few times.

For quite a while, I talked with those in charge of Dark-view's anarchic side. The thieves and beggars were well aware of what would happen if Doyle permanently established his rule. Peasants, merchants, nobles, and thieves would all suffer equally.

In a tyrannical state, thieves would be rounded up for 'public safety,' and after them, the dissidents would follow their friends into the dungeons.

What many kept bringing up was the castle's fortifications. The beggars knew that everyone and everything going through the gates was inspected thoroughly. The thieves had noticed the castle's escape tunnels were being guarded heavily, and the sewers beneath the citadel were carefully watched.

Slowly, but surely, prodding them on the potential fall-out of Doyle's rise to power, and counter balancing it with keeping the status-quo and their involvement hidden, I was able to breathe new life to their anger. The downtrodden and the misfits were usually easy to be directed, but to my surprise the speakers for each group took an effort to be guided toward the path to violence. They weighed our options. Slowly making our way into inside the castle would be near impossible. Bribing his officers might work, but was risky. Blackmail would potentially have a lot of options, but I personally dejected the solution. To be honest, I needed a distraction to draw the guard's attention while working my way inside.

Finally seeing a chance by noting to them about miti-gating the risk. If they draw the angry attention of the guard for a moment, I would put myself in danger. Surely it was better for me to work inside the castle, while they only had to draw attention, with little immediate risk onto themselves.

The beggars were the first to agree, but they looked uninterested. I hated to gamble, but I had to move things along.

"Well, you could take the time to loot some noble houses, while their guard moves to secure the castle. When you move to raiding and burning their houses, the nobility will have no choice but to pull their forces back to their own estates," I suggested. While greed was a usual motivator, it seemed the thieves were equally interested in just making the life of nobility a bit harder.

Taking the bait, the thieves were in, followed quickly by the disorganized group that I had hard time identifying. Perhaps they were a start of organized crime families in the area? Whoever they were, they seemed more interested in creating havock than anything else. When burning was added to the things done, their eyes suddenly lit, and their nodding began in earnest.

For the next hour, I was dragged from meeting to meeting as the spark of a rebellion was ignited. Spent and finally out of breath, I ducked into a small alleyway to catch a wink of shut-eye while the criminal minds of the city deliberated on what to do. Barely fifteen minutes passed before I was nudged awake by a curious man in chainmail wearing Doyle's regalia as well as his own. Groggily, I rose to my feet and waited for him to speak. He hadn't stabbed me yet, so he obviously had something to say.

"Edward, I believe. Don't move too much. Sir Alan said you could get quite jumpy. There are those in the castle who don't care much for Doyle. I wouldn't mind gaining an upper hand in certain arrangements after he is dealt with.

But we can talk about that later. Let's say you'll owe me. Give me your word to honor a reasonable request later." I nodded, not about to say that my decisions didn't matter, Brigit's did. "Now then, I might have a way of getting you inside the castle. If what I've heard from Sir Alan is true, you'll do fine." The man kept talking and talking...and talking. After a while I lifted a hand to make him stop his long-winded monologue.

"First of all, I want to know your name. Secondly, what is this way in?" I asked, keeping myself as calm as I could.

"My apologies. I'm Daniel Lemore. I forget you haven't been in Freehaven long. My way to get you inside is simple. You'll prove yourself combat worthy. There's a small tournament this evening to recruit even more disgruntled people to Doyle's growing army, using the kingdom's money," Daniel said with a smile in his voice.

Oh great, this man absolutely loves this idea. But there is a chance it might work.

Hashing out the plan with Daniel took an hour, during which he dragged me to a tavern to feed me while a bath was drawn for me. He insisted I thoroughly groom myself. Apparently a band of mercenaries were acting as officers, and he wanted me to take one of their positions.

As our plan came together, time began to run out. We made our way by carriage to the castle where fighting cages had been set up to test new contestants. Daniel whispered to me the entire time. He was quite the nervous talker.

I finally found myself waiting in a seat, overlooking a dirt and sand fighting pit. One-by-one aspirants were drawn down to the pit, to fight. First two fights were quick and brutal, as each was fought with claymores. While I knew my way around the blade, the quick full-body combat style they utilized was utterly alien to me. Kicks and grabs were as common as actual swings, reminding me again that I was not up-to-par with my know-how on how the locals fought.

The one after the two was a quick one. What seemed like a young noble was trying his epee against a brute of a man holding a warhammer. To the nobles benefit, he did manage to make two scoring wounds on the man, but his luck ran out when his epee broke against the hammer. The on-lookers sat impassive as the noble was pummeled to the ground, where he lay unmoving. It seemed the young man's trials were permanently over.

As his body was moved out to an unknown destination, I heard my name called out.

MY TURN CAME, and I was ready. Making my way down to the pit I told the organizer I preferred a short-sword. My opponent stepped in soon after. He was a burly butcher with arms as big around as my head. Thankfully, there wasn't much intelligence in his eyes. As soon as our weapons were handed to us, he lunged at me as if hoping for a quick kill. The swords we were given were a dull bronze, and I sneered at their condition. Perhaps the game masters wanted a combat of skills instead of having the losers outright killed.

Biding my time, I danced out of the butcher's way a few times, slicing into his arms and legs. The hefty man pushed on, unwilling to admit defeat. Time was running short, and the other cages had already been changed. "I'm sorry," I said under my breath.

He roared like a beast and lunged forward.

I clenched the sword in both hands, knowing what I needed to do. Resting the hilt against the heavy wooden support, I crouched at the last moment. Air exploded from my lungs as he smacked into me, but then he fell to the ground with the sword still in his chest. Blood trickled from the wound, and I pushed to my feet. Among the cheers around me, I heard the words I'd hoped for. "This one." One of the game masters above pointed to the cage I was in.

Relief lifted a weight off my shoulders, and it took restraint not to smile.

The winners as we were, we found that the organizer had rented a small tavern next to the testing venue and against the castle walls. It was close enough that I could almost smell the blood in the air. It mattered little as young wenches milled around, oblivious to our wounds and nicks, as they brought bread, vegetables and beer. The second around that soon followed had deer, beef and chicken prepared in various ways. I sat with a few others that had been chosen. One of them was overly eager and boasting of his kill on the field.

It took me a moment to recognize him as the warhammer user. Well, it mattered little to me. To avoid suspicion I jovially boasted my own achievement, shoving grief that the blade I had been given had been useless in my hands. Of course, it had the wanted effect, as more cheers and beer was shared. It didn't take long to notice that some of the newly drafted men were trying to woo one of the wenches for themselves. By the time the third new recruit had been cut by knives I barely saw the wenches carry the attempts grew a lot less eager. But apparently it didn't stop them from trying.

I spent the time eating, drinking and displaying the slow slope toward becoming drunken. Slurring the speech was the easy part, but I tried to keep the balance problems to the moment I began to head out to the streets for relieving myself.

On the way back, I spied a tunnel that seemed to extend into the castle. Sticking to the shadows, I made my way into the tunnels. They intersected many times, and it took me little while to find the section Daniel had told me about. The one pointed toward the kitchen.

The castle was like a multi-layered cake with the dungeons and darker aspects hidden in the floors below, then the servants, the kitchens, and the supply rooms. The guards and nobility stayed on the floors above. The more important prisoners were reportedly held in the Eastern Tower, facing away from the city. Following the route Daniel had drilled into my head, I took three staircases, two of them down and one up, to avoid most of the guards. The tunnels were below ground level, and the only lighting I had was from an occasional torch.

The heavy footsteps of the rare guard echoed in the tunnels, making it easy to avoid a confrontation with them. Ducking into a small alcove usually got me out of harm's way, but it made for slow progress. It took nearly half an hour before I saw the dark skies above. The weather appeared to be turning again. Lightning in the distance spoke of yet another storm heading for the city.

The next step was the most dangerous. Once outside on a small platform of stone, wood, and sand, I located the Eastern Tower. Guards walked around it, leaving my only option a route I'd hoped to avoid.

The inner courtyards, stables, and other buildings had roofs built to withstand projectiles from a catapult, but none of them were close by. Instead of relying on a purely athletic approach, I took my time and stuck to the shadows caused by their torches.

I pulled my cloak off and doused it with what little water I had left, hoping it was enough. Approaching one of the torches slowly, I remained at the edge of the light and waited. When my opportunity arrived, I quickly extinguished the flame with the sopping wet cloak. It would grant me a narrow window of time, and I took it. The guards would notice the flame having gone out in a moment, so I darted away and nearly sighed in relief as the guards who'd been in the way went to inspect the extinguished torch.

The climb would be long, but it might be the only way in. I was just happy it hadn't started raining yet. My hands were blistered before I even hit the halfway point where I had to take shelter from the strong winds. In my mind, it made things easier. No one would think to look at the outside of the tower for a suicidal rescue attempt. After a ten-minute break, the winds calmed a little, and I continued. Even so, a handful of times I nearly lost my grip on the smooth stones, but I eventually made it to a balcony of sorts. There were no guards, so I ducked inside the tower.

The balcony led to an old guardhouse intended for guards protecting the tower. The stairwell was quiet behind the door, so I opened it and continued up. Two levels later, there were a pair of torches on the wall, and a lone guard who'd fallen asleep leaning against the cold stone walls.

I slid my knife across his throat, dispatching him easily before I took his keys and opened the door beside him. A delicate shape curled up on the bed, apparently asleep. I dragged the guard's corpse inside and secured the door before jogging to the bed. Brigit looked so beautiful in her slumber. Her features were innocent, if a little bedraggled from the rough few days she'd had.

"Brigit, we have to escape before they know I'm here," I whispered quietly. It took a few moments of coaxing to get her to believe it was truly me.

Heavy thumping against the door drew our attention.

The room was a decent size, but it was no place for extended fighting. I brought out my gun and hoped the storm outside would mask the sound when I eventually used it.

The door broke apart as the men behind effortlessly chopped it to bits. As soon as I saw a helmeted face on the other side, I took a careful aim and shot him in the eye. He dropped out of sight, and there was a thud in the hallway. With a limited number of bullets left, I hoped I had enough.

"Sir Alan mentioned during his torture that you had some sort of toy with you. Shame you chose to be my opponent. I would have liked to know you, Edward. Kill him." A brooding voice came from the stairway as the men pushed into the room, four of them in total.

I shot two of them before they got close. The remaining two were armed with huge greatswords. The one on the left took a step forward, and I put a bullet in his torso. The other lunged at me with his sword, and I barely moved out of the way in time. The swordsman's momentum carried him too far, and he hit one of the nightstands nearby. Holding his arm, I shot him point blank in the face.

A man with extremely dark skin ducked into the room, throwing a dagger at me. Time slowed down as I used the merc's body as a shield and pulled the trigger. *Click.*

Bloody hell. Not now! The gun should've had half a clip left, but it had finally given up. The mechanism had jammed, and I didn't have time to clean it. The moment I'd look away, I would be an open target for him.

18

BRIGIT

Edward drew his sword and another from one of the dead mercenaries. Doyle swept his eyes to me, then back to his opponent. The two men in the room couldn't be more different. Edward was kindhearted, had helped someone he hadn't even known, and most importantly, he loved me. On the other hand, Doyle wanted to use me as a means to an end. He'd mercilessly sent hundreds, if not thousands, of men to secure the throne for his eventual heir.

The entire situation made my heart ache. I wanted it all to end. I wanted to be free and safe.

I took a sword from the barely cold corpse beside me and turned back to see both men glare at me. They fought brutally, blade striking blade, each picking up speed as the assault continued. Doyle was armored, but Edward only had light armor that seemed to do little to protect him from the cuts the men gave one another. While Edward had scratches here and there, Doyle had a long gash on his face. He'd been arrogant and unruly with his sword, but I knew it was unlikely Edward would score a similar hit anytime soon. While Doyle's armor kept him moving a little slower, he had more skill than Edward. Edward compensated with precise strikes, but sooner or later, their uneven skill would turn against him. The storm outside was building up momentum, and its electricity filled the air around us.

The lightning struck outside in time with the swords clashing, lighting the dark chamber with an eerie glow. Why couldn't my uncle just leave us alone? I threw my throwing dagger, and he effortlessly dodged out of the way. It barely missed Edward's extended arm as he reached in to slice the space where Doyle's arm had been moments before. The smell of sweat and blood permeated the room.

If I didn't do something, the man I loved would die.

A bolt of lightning hit the tower, causing it to shake a little and driving the men apart. They looked at one another warily before preparing for another barrage of violence.

"You're experienced, but you haven't trained long enough. The lunges and feints you use are too shallow. You seem to be afraid to die, moving away just before landing another cut," Doyle said, trying to goad Edward.

"You're one to talk. After all, you've barely harmed an unarmored man. Most of the scratches I have are from climbing up here. You get too cocky. Even if you live, whenever you look in the mirror, you'll always see that scar and know a better man did that." Edward's voice remained calm and detached, and his blue eyes reflected the lightning outside.

My heart leapt almost as fast as Doyle did. Edward slammed his forehead against Doyle's face, breaking his nose. Furious, Doyle ignored his pain and punched Edward in the ribs. There was an audible crack, but nothing reflected on Edward's face, even as a few drops of blood stained his lips.

My body burned from within. I couldn't watch him die. I looked down to see that my hands glowed bright red. As Doyle reached for him again, a loud boom came from the other side of the tower, throwing off his aim.

Edward seized the opportunity and kicked Doyle in the knee, then turned easily and landed a second kick to my uncle's chest. A loud snap reverberated through the room as Doyle's head hit the wall behind him.

Doyle threw a knife out from his right side that barely missed Edward's head. Edward widened his eyes and took a careful step back. There was little chance of him pushing further in the state he was in. While Doyle was heavily injured, his armor and helmet had saved him from the worst of the damage.

The men grew quiet, and I knew it had gotten serious. There was no taunting anymore. Both were fully committed to killing the other. The scratches on Edward's arms grew in number, while gouges were created in Doyle's armor.

Quicker than I could see, Doyle drew a dagger from his armor and barely managed to slice across Edward's knuckles. If he had leaned into the hit, he probably would've lost his arm.

Pulling back from the strike, Edward dropped the sword from his left hand. With two wide strikes intended to keep Doyle away, he used his injured hand to grab the edge of his torn cloak. He ripped it from his back. Instead of using it to wrap his hand, he whipped the edge of the cloak toward Doyle's eyes.

The trick worked two or three times before Doyle grabbed the edge of the cloak and pulled. Edward lost his footing and fell forward toward Doyle's sword. I screamed a warning, but it was too late. The blade was about to cut into his stomach when a blast of air from the balcony slammed into them. The blade barely nicked Edward, but I saw him flinch in pain. Instead of letting his momentum go to waste, he wrapped the fabric around Doyle's throat as they shuffled around on the floor. His side was bleeding, but the cut didn't seem to be deep.

I wanted to cry in relief, but I had a feeling the fight was still far from over.

Choking, Doyle cut the fabric between him and Edward, receiving two nasty cuts to his arms while doing so. "Bitch, do not interfere!" Doyle yelled at me, his eyes flashing angrily.

What did he mean? I'd merely yelled in surprise. I drank in the moment, and realized my body was still on fire, but it had changed. My energy still lingered in the room as tiny wisps. Had I caused that buffet of air?

Tentatively, I reached out, and a current of air moved around the room. What was this? I'd never felt my power like this. The fighting seemed to move in slow motion, as my mind worked overtime. The current of energy changed at a whim, my whim, and I had conscious control over it. It both scared and fascinated me.

Doyle had grown as pale as a drow could. He continued to fight Edward, but now his attention skipped between the two of us. He hesitated and paid the price as Edward's sword cut into his leg, piercing through the armor and leaving streaks of blood behind. He snarled as he refocused on his opponent and rammed his knee into Edward's cut side, just below the wound.

Losing his balance, Edward drew backward and lifted his sword up weakly, barely able to block the next blow Doyle sent his way.

Instead of closing in for the kill, Doyle stole a sideways glance at me and threw one of his knives in my direction. Instinctively, I focused the wisps of my energy before me like a shield, and it bounced to the floor in front of me.

Hatred burned in his red eyes as he took a step toward me, his blade raised in air. "When I open his flesh, know it's only because you love him. There he is, trying to get off the ground again. He's bleeding all over my tower and ruining the evening I was to have with you. Maybe I'll make you watch while I cut his throat." His vile suggestion hung in the air, making me want to puke. "Who knows, maybe I'll take that maid in front of you too. She screamed so much last night. You know what? You're nothing, Brigit. Nothing. Neither were your parents."

Thunder roared around us. How dare he? He'd killed my parents, tortured my friends and companions, and was trying to kill Edward and me. We weren't nothing. "I'm the princess of Freehaven. Remember your place, pretender. You do not have the crown or the throne. My people will rise against you. Those whose lives you ruined will have their revenge." As I spoke, I felt fury building inside me.

Doyle tried to take another step forward, but was stopped by another lightning bolt striking the tower. It was all so much to keep under control. The air shimmered with possibilities. I merely had to reach out with my mind and call down the power of the black skies above. It was addicting, intoxicating, and I didn't want to stop. "I want you gone, Doyle!" With a scream, I thrust my hand toward him as a gust of wind swept him off his feet and ripped him from the tower. His screams faded into the distance as he dropped to the courtyard below. A faint thud silenced his cries.

The joy and exhilaration of using my power faded into a

cold pang of sadness. My legs gave out, and I reached for Edward who caught me with a pained wince on his face.

"You're shaking, Brigit."

All the energy I'd possessed had been used up in the final thrust of my power. I could barely keep my head up. Before I slipped into darkness, I whispered two words. "Hold me."

19

BRIGIT

It had been a few months since the fight with Doyle. Things were slowly calming down as far as politics went. With Doyle dead and his bodyguards run out, the nobles fully accepted their rightful queen. Under the circumstances, no trial was being held, merely my coronation and a declaration that we wouldn't stand for tyranny in Freehaven.

My declaration to wed Edward stirred some controversy, but I didn't care. Many of the nobles and knights who had hopes for a spot at my table saw their dreams crushed.

As Edward recovered, I used the opportunity to gain more control over my powers and seek assistance in understanding my own limits. Magic, while usually weak in my kingdom, saw a small increase in users strengthening their power in our realm. That explained how I'd been able to do so much during the storm. But I had no idea how or why the magic had awakened in me to the degree that it had. Perhaps it knew I needed to save my true love.

Edward recovered well and offered to move around with

the troops to chase away any remaining mercenaries as we laid the defenders of Skyhaven to rest. Sir Alan had lit Sir Orlan's funeral pyre. The solemn occasion was an important one, and a reminder to all of their crucial sacrifices in holding back a tyrant who threatened the kingdom.

Tabitha became close with Sir Alan after their imprisonment, and now they were quite inseparable. I wouldn't have to issue a royal decree to marry him off after all.

As I arrived back to Darkview from visiting my dear cousin, Lord Flemming, I found Sir Alan and Edward were in the study talking. While they spoke, I had tea with Tabitha. She announced that she and her knight were expecting. Despite my happiness for them, Tabitha insisted I was not to share the news, as they wanted to marry before word of it spread too far. We would help plan the ceremony together.

"What about yours?" Tabitha asked and softly nudged my stomach.

At first, I didn't catch her meaning. I hadn't told anyone yet...not even Edward. I wanted to make sure before getting anyone's hopes up. How did she know? "Am I showing yet?" I asked, staring down at my torso.

"No, not yet. Well, you've gotten a little rounder, but I thought you were just recovering from what happened." Tabitha smiled at me. Humor, excitement, and a giddy happiness brightened her eyes. I was happy for her. She wasn't a maidservant anymore but a lady of the court. Was I jealous of Sir Alan for taking so much of her time now? Maybe. But they deserved one another and long, happy lives. I wasn't about to get in the way of that.

I excused myself and headed for the study.

Sir Alan was perusing books and scribbling notes, but

there was no sign of Edward. He bowed his head and gave me a quizzical look before saying the words I'd been dreading. "We finally have progress on the door, Your Majesty."

Edward had been seeking an answer on how to return to his world ever since he could get out of bed. It motivated him, and he spent much of his time digging through tomes that were barely legible anymore.

"Where is he?" I snapped, perhaps a little stronger than I'd wanted.

Sir Alan rose from his chair, and we headed through an extensive maze of tunnels beneath the castle. We followed strange markings on the wall that had mostly lost their meaning. Sir Alan kept some notes for his reference on which turns to take, but it still took a while to find Edward. He was far beneath the castle, in an expansive cave that opened into a dome. An unnatural glow came from the very rocks themselves, suffusing the dome in a soft blue light. Throughout the dome were arches with symbols etched above them and on the rocky floor itself.

Edward stood in the middle of it all. He waved me over. The very air in this room felt sacred, as if we were in a temple. Neither Sir Alan nor I made much sound as we walked over to him, taking in the details of the dome. As we neared, I became aware of the dome's true size. Filled with awe, I wrapped my arms around Edward, who had patiently waited for me in the center.

"My love, this is the place," he said as he ran his hand over my back. He nodded to a pedestal beside us. It had an arrangement that I recognized from old tomes in the library. The dome, the arches, and the outcrops all pointed toward the outer realms of the connected worlds. Directly in front of the pedestal was a smaller door inside a single, lonely arch. On the arch was a word written without flourish. *Gauntlet.* That was where my ancestors had once lived before the turbulences in that world had driven them to leave. Earth...

"You found it," I said, still amazed by the discovery. How many generations had passed without finding this place? My own family had lived in the castle above for centuries without realizing what was deep under our very feet. We'd always been told this was a network of catacombs built on the ruins of another city. "It's wonderful here. The possibilities are endless," I said quietly, but dread filled my chest. Would he return home now? Would I ever see him again?

Edward nodded, but a mix of emotions played on his face. He was excited, in awe, and...sad. This had been his goal ever since he first appeared in our world, and now he'd finally found it. "I can go home and tell everyone I'm okay. I miss it there sometimes," he said, staring at the door.

Sir Alan had walked farther along the row of arches, as if inspecting them for any signs of trouble. As soon as he was out of hearing range, I leaned forward to brush my lips against Edward's. "Don't go yet. What would I tell your son or daughter? They'd wonder where you were."

Edward pulled me to arm's length and blinked a few times. "You're... We're...?" He cleared his throat. "Earth can wait. I have you, and the beginnings of a family." He held me close and placed kisses against my temple. I could feel his heart thumping quickly in his chest. "I'm going to be a father." He nearly shook with excitement.

I took his hand, and we began the long walk back to the castle. "One day I want to see all of these wonders you keep telling me about," I said, flashing him a smile.

His reply easily carried through the tunnels. "Maybe one

day. Right now, I want you and nothing else. I love you, Brigit."

————

LOOKING for more Edge of Oblivion? Grab the next book, *The Thief's Gambit...*

AUTHOR'S NOTE

Thank you for reading *The Assassin's Mark*. We hope you enjoyed it!

Please consider leaving a review at the retailer's website or on Goodreads, even if it's a line or two. It truly helps!

If you're interested in being the first to know about our next releases, sign up for Sarah's newsletter.

ABOUT SARAH MÄKELÄ

New York Times & USA Today Bestselling Author Sarah Mäkelä loves her fiction dark, magical, and passionate. She is a paranormal romance author and a life-long paranormal fan who still sleeps with a night light. In her spare time, she reads sexy books, watches scary movies, and plays computer games with her husband. When she gets the chance, she loves traveling the world too.

- amazon.com/author/sarahmakela
- bookbub.com/authors/sarah-makela
- instagram.com/authorsarahmakela
- facebook.com/authorsarahmakela
- twitter.com/sarahmakela
- goodreads.com/sarahmakela
- pinterest.com/authorsarahmakela

ABOUT TAVIN SØREN

Tavin Søren is an urban fantasy author. He loves whiskey, has a sense of adventure, and enjoys learning about all things supernatural.

ALSO BY SARAH MÄKELÄ

The Amazon Chronicles Series

(New Adult Paranormal Romance)

Book 1: Jungle Heat

Book 2: Jungle Fire

Book 3: Jungle Blaze

Book 4: Jungle Burn

The Amazon Chronicles Collection

Hacked Investigations Series

(Futuristic Paranormal Romance)

Book 1: Techno Crazed

Book 2: Savage Bytes

Book 2.5: Internet Dating for Gnomes *

Book 3: Blacklist Rogue

Book 4: Digital Slave

Courts of Light and Dark

(New Adult Fantasy Romance)

Book 1: Captivated

Book 2: Surrendered

Standalones

Moonlit Feathers

Captive Moonlight

Vera's Christmas Elf

ALSO BY TAVIN SØREN

Edge of Oblivion

EXCERPT FOR THE THIEF'S GAMBIT

TIMOTHY

Vibrations on the nightstand shattered the last few moments of my sleep. The dark night peered from the curtains. I cursed under my breath. There was little point in fighting to reunite with sleep's warm embrace. London didn't sleep, and neither did those who required my services.

I picked up my mobile phone and cleared my throat before answering, despite the fact it would do little to hide my grogginess from the caller. An unknown number popped up on the screen, but only a handful of people would ring me at this ungodly hour. A grimace spread across my lips as I answered the call.

"Good evening, Timothy. We have another assignment for you, one that requires your immediate attention. If you take this, we might be willing to overlook your lack of payment last week." The man's dry, lackluster voice had a crisp accent. He'd never given me his name, never shared many details about my assignments either. He merely brought them to my attention and made sure I paid my debt.

Hallmarks of the city's darker elements were all too obvious, but what could I do? I owed the local mob boss more than I cared to admit. My old gambling habit had my back pressed tight against the wall, and I still paid for my wild and reckless youth.

"I'll do it," I replied, and the unnamed man on the other end of the line hung up.

Now I'd log into various websites and search for public postings in the adult and other less savory sections. Missed connections were very popular with my clients, but risky assignments were something my clientele didn't want to be associated with. Probably had something to do with recent notices about various three-letter agencies cracking down on this type of communication, driving everyone back to using older, tried and true methods.

I grabbed a cup of coffee before firing up my laptop. When the computer finished loading, I opened the browser and set off to find details on my newest job. It didn't take long to locate the assignment.

An old lady wanted the company of a young man who had previously helped her in a museum. Apparently, she had been quite taken by the gentleman's knowledge of the exhibit, especially the old Italian necklace that had been on display.

I chuckled to myself, still shaking the last vestiges of sleep from my mind. So, this 'old lady' wanted 'help' with the necklace, huh? Not very subtle, but if it made my clients feel more at ease that I'd understand the job... However, I hoped the person who created the listing would be less cheesy next time.

I flagged the posting as fraud and logged out.

My client would get an email notice about being flagged, the sign I had taken the job. No one would be the wiser. No face-to-face meetings to discuss things beforehand, strict anonymity, and, most importantly, full deniability.

A generalized search on the museums in the area revealed only one matching entry based on the item's description, the Royal Museum of Art. *Good.* At least there would be no confusion about what the client wanted. Nothing frustrated me more than stealing the wrong item. A mistake I tried my hardest not to make ever again.

On second thought, I rang my brother Sam. It nearly went to voicemail when he answered with his typical gruff tone. "What is it?"

A slight sting of jealousy tightened my chest. He'd been up enjoying his Saturday night, but I no longer had that luxury.

"Hey, Sam. I just wanted to let you know I got another job. My client wants an Italian artifact appraised as soon as possible. Seems he can't wait until tomorrow. It looks like I won't be making it to breakfast. Can I catch up with you another time?" I hoped he'd buy into my bullshit about the job. He respected what he thought I did. If he only knew...

Missing our weekly get-together bothered me. Our time to catch up on one another's lives started when I'd moved out on my own. Meeting with him meant a lot to me.

"Seriously, mate? You're always hunting for one piece of art or another. Some things are better left buried." He sighed in my ear. "But you've got a job to do. Just be careful. That major explosion wasn't long ago, and I'm afraid for our country. The MI6 agent still hasn't been found. He's most likely dead, or maybe terrorists abducted him. If it can happen to someone like that..." Sam cleared his throat. "Anyway, you can pick up the check next week." His dry humor almost managed to hide his disappointment, but I knew him too well.

"Fair, I'll pay for breakfast next time." I ran a hand through my sleep-tousled hair. "Don't worry about me. I might not be MI6, but I know how to take care of myself." My skills had kept me alive while dealing with the mob, but my brother didn't need to know that. "As for my job, I'll slow down when I can. I promise."

"Right. Text me if things change." He let out a loud yawn.

Unfortunately, I doubted they would. "Get some sleep." I ended the call and set my mobile on the desk.

Sam didn't know about my nightly excursions. The less he knew about the darker side of the world, the better. Our parents had died when we were young. Night terrors and mental issues plagued Sam ever since. If he knew I was working on the other side of the law, he'd lose it.

The explosion that took place a few weeks ago returned to my mind.

While driving home after lunch, a building ahead of us had exploded into flames. I barely had a chance to slam on the brakes. Debris plastered the windshield, putting several cracks in it. Sam went white with shock, shaking uncontrollably and refusing to speak with anyone for the rest of the day. It had broken me to see him like that.

I couldn't let him suffer again, but if I didn't do my job, the mob might come after him. They knew he was my one weakness. I shelved the uncomfortable thoughts and packed a few supplies into my backpack.

My old, reliable Toyota sputtered as the engine came to life. Most of my neighbors were used to my odd hours, so this departure would be ignored as another student partying late into the night. Sometimes I was glad to live near a university.

The motorway was empty at this time of night, but a

dense fog rolling through the area forced me to slow down. An annoyance maybe, but I embraced its presence. It reminded me just how much we didn't see of the real world.

I pulled into an unlit corner of the museum's parking lot. The street lamps did nothing to penetrate the fog, which would help me make a clean escape. The museum grounds had a few exhibits tied to the Italian Renaissance, including a collection of marble statues. They were obviously replicas, but their finely sculpted silhouettes managed to portray an air of authenticity.

Stalking through the mists was invigorating, and I relished the moment. The fog would help conceal my shape from any cameras and guards on the property, but it was better to be safe. I slid into my gear and donned a gray and white leather mask. It was old school, but at least I didn't need to worry about it falling off if I had to sprint through the trees to my car.

Sweeping trails of light shone across the yard from me. Instead of illuminating anything, the cone of light likely made it impossible for the guards to see anything in the fog.

Typical. Guess that's why I'm the thief.